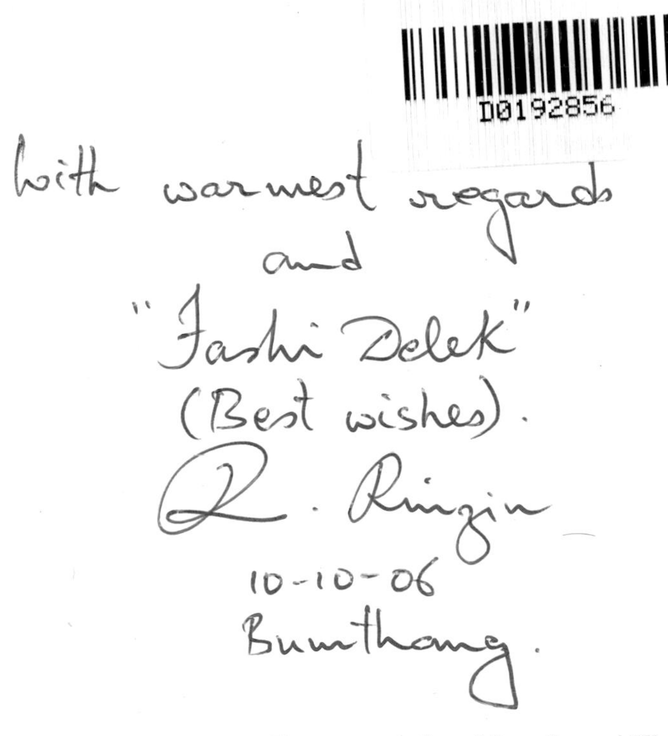


*For my mother Mrs. Jurmi Wangmo*
*and*
*sons Jigmi, Kuenphen, Lekden and Phuntsho*

# *The Talisman of Good Fortune*

*and*

*other stories from rural Bhutan*

*Rinzin Rinzin*

First 1500 copies published with support from Helvetas/SDC in
October 2002.

**Distributed by:**

Mrs. Sonam Wangmo,
Kurtoe Handicraft Shop,
Yarkay Central,
Pox Box No. 685,
Thimphu, Bhutan.
Tel. No. (00975)-02-324642/325883
Mobile No: 17603694

&

Mrs. Kelzang Wangmo Rinzin
Bumthang Handicraft Shop,
Chamkhar Town,
Bumthang, Bhutan.
Tel. No. (00975)-03-631405/631322
Mobile No.: 17600303

Printed at Kuensel Corporation, Thimphu, Bhutan.

Illustrations by Lydia Wespi

Layout and typeset by Markus Wespi

**ISBN: 99936-619-0-2**

---

# *Table of content*

# *Introduction*

Ever since I was a child, I was always fascinated by the eerie tales about the *Du Ginmee* (Poison Givers), *Soendrey* (Evil Spirits of the living), *Nyenpa* or *Nyen Tangmee* (The one who casts evil spells on others). Kurtoe Goenpakap, my birthplace, like many other places in Bhutan, is a place where people have strong believes in the existence of such paranormal things. People conducting rituals to neutralise the affects of such things is as common as the *Tshechu* and other annual festival celebrations in both rural and urban Bhutan. Besides, directly or indirectly accusing those who are believed to possess such supernatural powers of making a person sick and or ending a person's life is quite normal. I have been a witness to such rituals on various occasions during my early childhood in Kurtoe and else where. Furthermore, at the age of six, I was myself treated by a shaman, Late *Pao* Kezang, for having apparently taken poison from a Poison Giver. Therefore, as a child, I was even afraid of being anywhere near those people who were believed to be either a *Du Ginmee* or a *Nyen Tangmee* or of having the *Soendrey* in them. However, the subject of such nature have always intrigued me and risen many questions in me. As a scholar of applied science, I sometimes find such paranormal things highly irrational. At the same time, coming from a rural Bhutanese family and living in Bumthang where people believe in paranormal activities as much as my village folks do, they never fail to fascinate me. However, I cannot help but feel sorry particularly for those who are believed to be *Du Ginmee* or of having *Soendrey* (I will not attempt to reason why, but leave it to you to make your own judgement!). *The talisman of good fortune*, *The avenger's day* and *The devilish inheritance* are stories revolving around such subjects.

Then, we have different spirits of all sorts who are believed to harm us in equally different ways. We believe that even some of our own guardian deities harm us if we angered Him or Her in any way or failed to appease Him or Her. Such beliefs and traditions have been a part of my life, and inspired me in superficially touching them while writing some of the stories (like *The clandestine foes*.)

My village folk's efforts in sustaining goodwill in my village and living in harmony with one another and the environment are typical of a lay Buddhist's life. I have tried to present the tip of the iceberg of such perseverance of goodwill through *New legacy for a village*.

My mother once told me that the presence of a responsible man in one's family is a necessity as far as the family's social status is concerned, especially in rural Bhutan. May be in some distant villages it is still so- much more than in modern Bhutanese or western families. Through the fictions of *Wild mushrooms for mother* and *Samphel's pride and woes*, I have tried to relate my own experiences in this field, and present the reader with a vivid picture of my mother's and many other women's belief. I must, however, caution you that this has no bearing to my being a man what-so-ever.

We often encounter people with different kinds of obsessions in their lives, the degree of an obsession varying markedly from person to person. I am no different from them. Nevertheless, I often wonder how far one's obsessions can go. *Apa Nadola's obsession* is a result of my own amazement at such obsessions in life.

Life in Kurtoe in particular and rural Bhutan in general has changed very fast during the last 25 years or so. Sadly enough, I have not had the pleasure of witnessing the changes that took place in Goenpakap since I have been away at Thimphu and elsewhere since 1981. I hear from my parents and my village folks that Goenpakap wears a different look now. Therefore, I get a feeling that tomorrow if I should visit it, it will not be the way I have always remembered it. Hence, much as I like to bask in the sunshine of modern Bhutan, I think I will always miss good old Goenpakap of early 1970s. *Maymay Wamla's umbrella* is a line to the Goenpakap of my childhood days.

I have written these stories based on my personal experiences on the widely believed and talked about but least written side of the rural Bhutanese life. However, it was not my intention to pass judgement on any of the beliefs and events presented in these stories. Furthermore, although most of the events presented in my stories reflect true happenings in rural Bhutanese society, all the names of persons and places in the stories are fictitious.

Happy reading!

Rinzin Rinzin
Jakar, 30th September 2002

# Acknowledgement

I must sincerely acknowledge Mr. Marcus Wespi and Mrs. Lydia Wespi for taking personal interest in my manuscript and voluntarily working on the layout and illustrations, and exploring for funds to publish my manuscript. The time they have spared in reading my manuscript and the kind words of encouragement they have given me shall remain in my heart forever.

My thanks are due to Ashi Kunzang Choden, author of Bhutanese Tales of the Yeti and Folk Tales of Bhutan, for taking time to go through some of my stories and for providing constructive criticism and valuable suggestions.

I am also grateful to Todd Asuncion and his wife Bec, Mr. Phuntsho Norbu, Nima Yoeser, Mr. Chimi Dorji and Mr. Kuenga Tshering for sparing their time to read my stories, for their valuable comments and for their warm friendship in Melbourne.

My sincere gratitude and acknowledgement are also due to Dr. Tashi Dorji and Late Mr. Bal B. Pradhan for letting me use their laptops to work on the stories during the many holidays and weekends in Bhutan, and Mr. Nima Yoeser for the same during the winter break in 2001 in Australia. If it had not been for their laptops, it would not have been possible for me to make those many holidays, weekends and the winter vacation full-time working days for me, and realise my dream of publishing my stories in a predetermined time.

I owe my sincere thanks to Mr. Dieter Zurcher for sparing his valuable time in reading my manuscript, and to SDC/Helvetas, Bhutan Programme for providing funds to publish my stories.

I owe a lot to my wife Kezang, sons Jigmi, Kuenphen, Lekden and Phuntsho, sister Sonam and her husband Lhatu, aunts Kinley and Jambay, and my father Rinzinla (alias Rinzin Dorji) for believing in me.

Finally, I would like to dedicate my book to my mother for being the source of my inspiration.

# *The talisman of good fortune*

"What are you doing all alone by yourself, Tenzin?" asked the tall lady sweetly with the voice of an angle, bowing over the little boy who was digging into a crevice of a rock with a blunt stick outside Dolma's house.

"Playing!" answered the four-year old boy without looking at her, and continued to dig.

The lady casually looked around. When she was sure that there was nobody around, she took out a crunchy golden apple from the front pouch of her dress and gave it to Tenzin. The boy accepted it eagerly, and put it in the front pouch of his garment, too shy to eat it in her presence.

"What are you doing, Tenzin!" exclaimed the lady. "Eat it now. You don't want other kids to snatch it away from you, do you?"

At this the boy took out the apple from his pouch, held it with both hands and sunk his milk teeth into it.

"Smart boy!" praised the lady with a sly smile at the corner of her thick dark lipped mouth.

She loved giving small children the things they loved to eat. So, she would make sure that she always had 'a bit of something nice to eat' in her pouch every time she left her place. Her eyes scanned the surroundings again. Nobody was in sight.

"Eat it all up before someone gets here," she encouraged the boy who was taking a large mouth-full every time he took a bite, and munching on greedily. "Don't tell anybody that I gave you an apple," whispered the lady into Tenzin's little ear. "That was the last piece I had. I don't want the other children running after me asking for more, you see," she convinced the boy. "If you tell anybody about it, I will not give you the delicious peaches I have got at home!" warned the lady.

"I won't tell anyone," promised Tenzin with a serious look on his face, in an even lower whisper imitating the lady. "Not even my mother."

"Good boy!" said the lady and squired away.

Lhamo reached back home a happier woman that late afternoon. She had nothing to fear of anymore, at least not for a while. Hopefully, Tenzin the four-year old boy was going to save her life if Nagphey, the village shaman, did not get better of her. She recalled that the last time she had managed to give a child something to eat from her hand, *Pao* Pema had gotten better of her. She took out a *bangchu* of crispy beaten maize that she had fried in cow's butter before going out that morning. Then, she sat near the oven to prepare some salted butter tea. When the pot of tea was about to boil, she walked over to the kitchen window lethargically and looked out of the large wooden window."*Ama! Wai ama!* Come and have tea!" she called her mother in advance so that the tea does not get cold as she waits for her mother to walk slowly up the field, wash her soil-ridden hand and sit down for the tea.

"*Ya, ya!* I will," responded a frail voice from within a thicket of tall maize wavering gaily in the late afternoon breeze.

As she waited for the pot of tea to boil, she realised how utterly lonely and peaceful her house was. Her house stood alone at the edge of the forest, half way from all the surrounding villages that were way out of view from her house. Her mind went back to the day, sixteen years ago, when her grandmother had told her how their ancestors had been banished from their home about a century ago by their own village folks. The village folks had set their ancestral almost palatial house on fire, built a shabby house at the present location and dumped her ancestors into it after forbidding them to ever return to their ancestral home. Her banished ancestors had rebuilt the present house later. She could not remember when was the last time she had sat at a meal in her house with more than three people. It was said that since the time of her great grandmother, every men, women and children in the adjacent villages avoided the members of her family. Since then, they had never been invited to any of the annual household ceremonies hoisted in great pomp by every household in every village to appease the local guardian deities. Her grandmother had forsaken their part of the celebrations since no lay monks would come to their house to conduct the ceremonies.

"I have had enough of this insult," her grandmother had told her mother fuming with anger after the last lay monk had turned down her request to be one of the monks to conduct her family's ceremonies. "If it be the Guardian Deity Pelden Lhamo's will that we get no lay monks to help us appease her, so be it. Henceforth, this family shall not celebrate the annual ceremony, at least not as long as I am alive," she had sworn.

That was way before she was born. Therefore, she had never had the pleasure of being a part of such a celebration in her life, and she did not expect the story to change either. They never received visitors either. Even a tired and thirsty traveller passing by their house would try to sneak away although they always had a big earthen pot full of ice cold buttermilk or whey and fresh delicious cucumbers even in late winters to offer. The only person who dropped by occasionally was the village shaman who would just be too happy to eat and drink to his heart's content at the expense of their family. But then, he had his own reasons. He was the only man in the five nearby villages put together who had mastered the sacred spell at the mare utterance of which any ill affects of a food taken from a cursed soul could be neutralised. The family did not seem to mind much any-way. As for the others, everybody was just too scared to eat or drink anything from the hands of a member of their family. They were even scared of being touched by them. After all, theirs was a cursed family. They were the Poison Givers.

Just then, some tea boiled over onto the fire in the oven. The red-hot charcoal in the oven hissed and sent out clouds of ash-ridden dust as the tea choked the fire to death. Lhamo woke up with a startle from her daydream. She hurriedly took out a long piece of half burnt firewood and started to comb out the rest of the firewood and some red-hot coal with it from inside the oven to reduce the temperature of the intensely boiling tea. Then, she brought out an old lidless wooden churner from the corner of the kitchen room, put a filter on it and poured the pot of hot tea into it. She reached out on to the soot-ridden shelve near the oven for a wooden container of rancid butter. She scooped a generous amount of the butter from the container with a wooden ladle and dipped the tip of the wooden ladle with the butter into the tea. She stirred the hot tea with the ladle to wash the butter off it. Then, she took a scoop of salt from another wooden container with the same ladle and washed the ladle in the hot tea again. Then, as she started to churn the tea, memories long gone came back to her again.

She was only eighteen when Tshering, the man of her dreams who had robbed her of her virginity and impregnated her with Seldon had declined to marry her.

"Lhamo, it is true that I love you with all my heart, and I know that you love me too. But I cannot marry you, not even if you are carrying my child," Tshering had declared to her.

"But why?" she had cried clinging to him.

"Because... because you are a Poison Giver's daughter," he had replied sadly turning away his face from her to avoid eye contact with her. "My family will never accept you as their daughter in-law no matter what," he had concluded.

"But it is not true. My mother is not what you call her. You know that it is just a bad rumour, don't you?" she had tried to convince her lover.

"Please try to understand me, Lhamo. I am from a decent and humble family. My family has nothing but its pride to live with. I cannot destroy that pride by marrying you. I don't want my family and friends to disown me for marrying you," Tshering had tried to explain, to her utmost disappointment and embarrassment.

She had stood there alone dumbfounded, with her hand pressed against her shearing heart, and her eyes and mouth wide open. Just then, Tshering had shaken her hand off him and walked away leaving her alone to face the world. Then, as she had fumbled for words to call after him, her throat had gone dry and a cloud of darkness had engulfed her whole self, making every nerve in her body grow weak. Finally, she had slumped onto the dusty ground as if a totally emaciated starving bitch had been stuck by a lightening. After regaining her consciousness, she had hurried home in a cacophony of desperate cries and crazy laughter to the refuge of her mother and grandmother with the hope that they would prove Tshering wrong. She had stormed into her house like a rabid dog ready to bite anything in her way, and related what had happened to her to her grandmother.

"Sit down by my side, and calm down. I will tell you something which your mother or I should have told you years ago," her grandmother had calmly said after having heard her discourse.

"What do you mean, *aie*?" Lhamo had screamed into the old woman's face.

Just then, her mother had walked in and confused her even more by saying, "Is it already time, *ama*?" as casually as greeting a friendly neighbour.

"Yes, it is time. It is time Lhamo knows everything. She is only seventeen, but she is in trouble," her grandmother had replied making her head spin as if hit hard by an oak hammer.

A splash of hot tea washed over her left hand that was holding the churner, and she was body and mind in her kitchen again. She wiped her hand with the edge of her dress carelessly as if she did not feel the pain of the burnt on her hand. And just as she was transferring the well-churned tea into an aluminium teapot, her grey haired mother walked in with a sickle in her hand.

"I have been weeding the beans in the maize field," she announced. "The beans have already started to climb the maize plants. I think we are going to have a good harvest this year too."

She stuck the pointed end of the sickle into a crack on the pillar near the kitchen door, and slowly walked over to the oven. There she sat beside the fire and started to dry her wrinkled hands by exposing them to the heat of the fire. Lhamo carefully poured two drops of the salted butter tea from the teapot onto the palm of her left hand, licked the tea off her palm to taste for salt concentration. When she was satisfied that the tea had just about the right concentration of salt, she filled a large maple cup to the brim with it and passed the cup to her mother.

"I have been to Shamling," said Lhamo blankly.

"I know," her mother replied. "Have you had any luck?" she asked.

"I think so!" Lhamo hesitated, paused momentarily and continued, "I have managed to give an apple to Dolma's son Tenzin."

"That will do," retorted the old lady. "It will leave us in peace for a while."

Lately none of them have been able to make anybody eat or drink anything from their hands, and the silver cauldron in their altar room had been taking their sleeps away by making a lot of clanking noises from dusk till dawn every day. And they knew that the noise meant only one thing- the death of either one of them if they failed to please the curse. And the only way to please the curse was to successfully kill a person by offering poison to him or her.

As Lhamo and her mother sipped tea quietly without exchanging any conversation, Lhamo was again lost in memories. It had all started during her great-great grandmother Taumo's time, her grand mother Kardungmo had told her that day when Tshering had dumped her. The story went that during one of Taumo's trips to Lhasa, she had one day come across a young lonely Tibetan traveller at Kharchu, the first Tibetan settlement after crossing the Bhutan-Tibet boarder north east of Lhuntse. Since they were both headed to Lhasa, they had agreed to make the rest of the journey together. While on the journey, the two had become infatuated with one another. After several days and nights together, the young traveller had met a sudden death in Taumo's arms one unfortunate night. Nevertheless, just before he breathed his last, he had given Taumo a beautifully curved gold-coated silver cauldron filled to the brim with silver coins as a token of his love for her. He had told her that it was a talisman of good fortune and that she must never part with it. However, he had warned that the one who possesses the talisman must not spend or give away even a single coin from the cauldron. Spending or giving away even a single coin by the owner or any other person, he had warned, would release an incurable curse. He had died before he could tell her what the curse really was.

Nine months after Taumo's return from Lhasa, she had given birth to a beautiful daughter, Dolkar, Kardungmo's mother. Thereafter, she had remained a spinster the rest of her life, making a trip to Lhasa every year till Dolkar was old enough to carry on the family's business. By then, Taumo had already become the richest lady in her district. All those years, Taumo had kept the talisman neatly wrapped up in a large white beautiful ceremonial scarf made of silk that she had once bought in Lhasa at a cost of one silver coin, and secretly hidden at the back of the main altar in the alter room. She had not told about it to a single soul in the fear that somebody might try to steal it from her. Then, one day Taumo had left on a year long pilgrimage to Chorten Kora in Trashiyangtsi, Jampe Lhakhang, Kurjee Lhakhang, Tamshing Lhakhang and Mebartsho in Bumthang, Taktsang, Bumdra, Kichu Lhakhang, Dungtsi Lhakang and Ja Karpo in Paro and all the way to Bodhgaya and Varanasi in India. One day, while Taumo was still away on pilgrimage, her daughter Dolkar had accidentally come across the cauldron while cleaning the altar. After a few days,

Dolkar had left for Lhasa. Nevertheless, with four silver coins from the cauldron. Just about the same time, Taumo who was by then at Varanasi had visited a great *lama* who, after blessing her had had cautioned her saying, "You should have told about the cauldron to at least your daughter," taking her by surprise. Clairvoyance!

In the meanwhile, back in Lhasa Dolkar had bought a pair of large beautiful turquoises, which were as blue as the cloudless sky on a sunny summer day, and a pair of corrals that were as red as the petals of a fully bloomed red with the silver coins from a Tibetan jeweller. That very night, a young handsome Tibetan man with a sad face had appeared in Dolkar's dream and said, "Dolkar, you should have consulted your mother before taking the coins from the cauldron and spending them. Now that you have parted with the coins, the curse has been released upon yourself and your mother and all your descendants to come." Then, the man in her dream had had gone down on all his four and started to cry pathetically at the top of his voice. As he continued crying, with his face on the dusty ground as if to gag himself with the very dust of the ground he was lying on, she had sat up wide-awake in her bed sweating and panting. Just then, the clear starry Lhasan night around her host's house had been filled with a cacophony of barking dogs and crying jackals. And as her thick yak-hair's mattress had started to drench in her sweat in the chilling Lhasan night, her host had come into her room with a yak's fat lamp murmuring, "*Dendray gi tendrel nyenpa!*" almost giving her a heart attack.

"Are you all right, *Drukpa bumo*?" he had asked seeing her awake and sweating in her bed.

Early next morning, Dolkar, being a superstitious lady, had gone out and combed the whole of Lhasa town in search of the jeweller. However, to her utmost disappointment, nobody had known a jeweller that fitted the description she had given. The jeweller seemed to have vanished into Lhasa's thin air, and with him the turquoises and the corrals from around her neck as well.

Well, it had not been only Dolkar who had had a bad night that fateful night. Back home, the whole village had been woken, at around the same time Dolkar was sitting in her bed sweating and trembling in Lhasa, by the eerie barking and crying of every single dog in the village. The dogs had behaved as if they were either at war with their close relatives the wolves or as if they were complaining against the arrival of the messenger of death who had just brought them the bad news that all the dogs in the village must die that very night. It was also said that some villagers had even seen an owl hovering round and round Dolkar's house and hooting frantically as if she was under threat from a force unknown to keep hooting till she woke up every man, woman and child in the village. Furthermore, to the horror of everyone, there was a chicken, a horse, a cow, a calf, a bullock, a donkey or a pig dead in every household in the village the next morning. Yes, in every household, except that of Dolkar's. That very day, anticipating the worst and with the hope of balancing the forces of nature by performing whatever religious rituals had to be performed, the village elders had consulted the village astrologer about the bad omen. And to the horror of all, the astrologer had prophesied that a curse had been released in one of the families in their village the previous day, and soon the curse would take a lot of lives not only from their own village but also from the villages far and wide. "There is also no known ritual that can either neutralise or destroy the curse. Now, all we can do is to put our faith in the Three Jewels and pray to them to protect us," he had added bluntly but honestly as per his calculations and predictions that corresponded with the consultations to his most trusted and over used hand-written scripture of astronomy. All the village elders had known too well, through their long associations with the astrologer, that the astrologer's predictions seldom went astray. Therefore, the horrified and helpless elders had immediately resorted to counteract the predictions by following the astrologer's advise by reciting the prayer of refuge in the Three Jewels one hundred million times in the village monastery by pulling together the necessary resources like food and manpower from within the village.

After Dolkar was back home from that trip, she had tried to replace the four silver coins that she had taken from the cauldron with her own. When she took out the cauldron from behind the main alter, unfolded it and tried to replace the coins, to her awe she had seen that the cauldron was still full to the brim, just the way it was before she had removed the four coins. Of course, since both Dolkar and her mother had never counted the coins in the cauldron, there was no telling if the four silver coins that Dolkar had spent in Lhasa had returned to the cauldron of their own accord! Nevertheless, Dolkar and her mother had believed that they had. Besides, strangely enough, the very Tibetan jeweller had appeared in Dolkar's dream the night she tried to replace the coins. It was said that the jeweller had just stared at Dolkar for a long time and then he had pointed his long brown index finger at her, and laughed and laughed at the top of his voice till she woke up screaming in the middle of the night.

After Taumo had heard about the eerie things that had happened at home and at Lhasa after Dolkar had spent the silver coins, she had taken the cauldron to the Kurichu River about two hours' walk from her village, and had thrown it into the middle of the river. To her awe and horror, instead of sinking the cauldron had floated in the river as if it were a feather. She had even rubbed her eyes to make sure that she was not seeing things. However, against her expectation the cauldron had floated towards the bank of the turbulent river, where she was standing, and had slide safely onto the dry sand as if it had legs of its own. No, not legs but wings! Furthermore, it had not left any mark on the sand as if it had landed there from the sky, and it was as dry as a flame without even a drop of water on or inside it. Also not even a single coin had seemed to have moved or fallen off the cauldron. Then, Taumo had frantically tied a rock to the cauldron and flung it into the river again. Then, like a woman who had just seen a ghost, her face pale and white with no signs of blood in it and her gait irregular and unbalanced like that of a rabid dog, she had left the riverbank without even bothering to look back and see if the cauldron had actually sunk in the river. When she had reached back home and had sat beside the oven to cook, her had her heart in her throat and her eyes had opened so wide that they had ached with strain. The cauldron had been lying beside her earthen curry pot near the oven. Desperate to get rid of it, she had even tried to burn it, but the cauldron had remained as cold as an unsheathed sword on a frost covered stone slab outside her house on a January morning even after it had been placed on a heap of white-hot coals for half a day. Ever since, the cauldron had remained with their family, and with it the curse.

"I am sorry, Lhamo, but this is the way it is! We have no choice but to accept the curse," Kardungmo had told her.

"But why do people call you and mother Poison Givers?" Lhamo had asked still crying.

"Because the Poison is the curse. Anybody, except the members of our own family, who eats or drinks from our hands gets it. This is why people call us the Poison Givers," her grandmother had explained.

"*Lama kheno!*" she had cried even more. "If people get poisoned by us only if they eat or drink from our hands, why do we have to offer them anything to eat or drink at all?" she had challenged.

"Because if we don't, the curse will force us to give it to one of our own, including our own children or parents," she had replied with a heavy sigh.

"What if you don't give it to your own people either?" she had inquired further.

"The curse will force you to give it to yourself, and kill you," had been the straightforward answer.

"It is better to kill oneself than kill others or one's own!" she had challenged her grandmother again.

"But what use is killing oneself when you know that the curse is not going to go away anyway! What use is killing one's own child or parent when you know that the curse can be kept from doing harm to her and oneself as long as you keep giving the poison to others!" her grandmother had reasoned sounding like a tired Yogi. "Even if we give away the cauldron to someone else, the curse will live one. It will only be another person or family who will live the cursed life. We are all humans, and we are all alike in our needs and desires. Everybody loves to live a long, happy and comfortable life. With the curse, the immediate members of our family live longer and more comfortable lives. Of course, social conflicts do make us unhappy sometimes, but my dear, happiness is in one's own heart," she had concluded managing to confuse her completely.

"But how do you give the poison? I mean what is it?" Lhamo had asked too confused to argue with her grandmother any further.

"It is nothing material. You cannot see it. You cannot smell it. You cannot feel it. You cannot hear it. It is but just a curse. All you know is that it is with you once you have inherited it," Kardungmo had put it as simple as she could. "So, you see, there is actually nothing poisonous for us to give to others. We just offer things to eat and drink, and when they take what we offer, they just get it," she explained adding, "Of course, not all of them are affected by our poison. I guess there are always some lucky stars even amongst the ordinary."

"I don't understand! How do you know that you have inherited it?" Lhamo had asked curiously trying to enlighten herself only on the issues that directly concerned her.

"When more and more people die after they had either eaten or drunk from your hands," Kardungmo had replied, the signs of subconscious guilt and conscious sadness clear in the tone of her voice and the collecting tears in her old eyes.

"But... but people could die of anything!" Lhamo had argued bluntly but with a pinch of rationality in it.

"Not the way they die from our poison," the old lady had answered almost confidently. "No medicine can cure one who suffers due to our poison. Medicine will only make the poison stronger. So far, there is only one man, Nagphey, the village shaman, I know of who knows the art of treating a person who is affected by our poison. Even he will fall prey to our poison one of these days.

One of these days, he is bound to forget to secretly chant his sacred spell, and he will..."

"*Aie*, you sound as if you..." Lhamo had screamed at her grandmother with disgust interrupting her and stopping her from uttering something highly sinful.

"Yes, he must die or our lives will be in peril!" Now it had been the grandmother's turn to ignore Lhamo's protest and stop her from heaping accusations of any kind on her.

"What do you mean?" had been yet another query of utmost surprise from Lhamo.

"The more people he saves from our poison, the more pressure we will be under from the curse to kill one of our own. The curse is such that we must keep on giving the poison to others. It is said that my grandmother Taumo was a very religious lady. However, after the release of the curse, many village people who had had food or drinks from her hands had died. Within just one and a half years' time, the village people had accused her of being a Poison Giver and of having killed at least seven people. Then when she realised that the curse was the poison, she had refused to give it to anybody, and the curse eventually taken her own life. She had died of the same symptoms as those who had died of her poison, and everybody in the village had known that her own poison had killed her when she had failed to give it to others. And my father had died from my mother Dolkar's poison when she had stopped giving it to others," Kardungmo had explained convincing Lhamo.

"Is there a way to escape from the curse?" she had asked hopefully but desperately trying to measure ways to escape from the curse.

"Not one anybody knows of," had been the hope-shattering answer. When Lhamo had let our her despair in a torrent of tears, the old lady, with the understanding that surely befitted the scores of years that she had been an occupant on mother earth exclaimed, "And why would you want to escape from it in the first place!" Then, she had lovingly caressed her dear grand daughter's long silky hair and continued, "The curse protects our family and gives us wealth and power. People may shun us for what we are, but they dare not harm us or insult us in the face in the fear that even if they themselves could keep away, their children or relatives would eventually fall victims to our poison," her grandmother had reasoned with a sense of great pride in her possession.

"But, Tshering has just dumped me for that!" Lhamo had countered with a confused mind but trying to keep track of the main purpose of the discussion.

"And no one will dare steal anything from us even if we keep our doors open without any guard, in the fear that they would inherit the curse through the very thing they steal from us," the old lady had continued as if she had not heard even a word of Lhamo's remark.

Then, the old lady had taken a deep breath after which she had exhaled a long sigh and dumbly exclaimed, "Has he!" She had chuckled, shook her head as if trying to wake herself up from an unwanted sleep, and exclaimed again, "So you are already aware that no man would dare marry into our family!" She had spared Lhamo a slow lethargic glance and broke into a ghostly laughter. Lhamo had felt the hairs on her body rise, as her grandmother's eerie laughter filled the house.

"*Aie!*" Lhamo had murmured through her quivering lips with her wide open eyes fixed on the old lady.

After a while that seemed like eternity to Lhamo, the old lady had stopped laughing abruptly. She had cleaned the tears off her brown wrinkled face with the edge of her *tegu* that had not been laundered for ages in a row.

Then, holding Lhamo's right hand with her rough and thick skinned hand, yet another undisputable evidence of her lengthy dealing with the ways of the world, had said in a soft staggering voice, "Lhamo, my child, what Tshering has done to you is nothing to be surprised of. Nor is it something that you let you hurt your feelings. This was bound to happen anyway, at least to the ladies in our family," unfolding yet another secret to Lhamo.

"But, *Aie...*" Lhamo had tried to say something but the words had failed to come to her lips.

"The same had happened to me and your mother, you see," the old lady had said as if to console Lhamo. Then, to Lhamo's surprise, her grand mother had added, "It is just that the children they fathered to other women never survive. And ultimately even their wives widow them, and no other women would marry them either." Her grand mother had burst into uncontrollable laughter again till tears rolled down her eyes and both her hands were holding her belly. Her own mother had joined the laughter surprising Lhamo even more.

"But *Aie*, I am carrying his child!" Lhamo had complained.

"So were we in our own times," her mother had retaliated and joined the conversation after a long last. "Don't worry. At least you will have a daughter by your side to take care of your in your old days. We always give birth to daughters, you see. It comes with the curse too, I should think," she had added confidently. "And I must say that this is not bad at all either. Afterall, what good are the sons! They either look for a wife and go away or bring home a stranger with whom you have had nothing to do at all till the day she walks into your house to become the mistress of your own home," she continued. "I for one am in fact thankful to the curse to have always given us daughters," she added reassuring Lhamo.

The three ladies had continued their conversation all through the night. Lhamo had had a lot of mixed feelings about everything that they had discussed, but in the end she had known what to do. And, over the last sixteen years, she had poisoned every child Tshering had fathered and every young couple in the surrounding villages. Some had been saved time and again by *Pao* Nagphey's son Pema, also a shaman who had learned a great deal from his father. However, most had not been as lucky. Even Pema himself had been saved by his own father on two occasions after Lhamo and her mother had successfully poisoned him. Nevertheless, one fine night Nagphey had visited their house after having performed some rituals in a neighbouring village. Since he was already drunk when he reached their house, he had readily drunk some more *ara* from her mother's seemingly loving hands. And he had surely forgotten to secretly utter his scared spells, just like her grandmother had said, for that had been the last time he ever spent a night with her mother or visited their house. And since then, something had always told Lhamo that *Pao* Pema was attracted to her, and that soon he would also make the same mistake. She had also secretly taken a vow to poison Tshering's wife somehow so that Tshering would have to remain a widower for the rest of his life, just like her grandfather and her father. She had argued with her conscience that if she could not live a happy life, there was no reason why others should.... "Drink your tea before it gets cold," came a familiar voice from a distance. "Lhamo, what are you dreaming of?" inquired the voice, and then at an instant she was again body and soul in her kitchen having tea with her old mother.

"Nothing, mother," lied Lhamo. She picked up her wooden cup full of *suja* and slowly sipped at it.

"Are you going to join me in weeding the maize field tomorrow or are you planning to go some place?" asked her mother.

"No, I am not going any where," replied Lhamo. "I will finish up the weeding. You do the cooking," she suggested.

"That's good," responded the mother cheerfully. "My old bones can hardly cope up with the ways of the world, I must say," she added, and continued to sip her tea.

Well, that was just about the end of their conversation. Somehow, the two would hardly converse much with one another. Whenever they were together, may it be in the same room or in the same field, each would just keep herself occupied with one thing or the other to do, and speak to the other only when it was really necessary. So, one can just guess how lonely a life they lived. This was mainly because of the fact that Lhamo would shut herself off from the world around her.

Tshering and four other men had spent the last two days carrying firewood on their backs from a nearby forest on the outskirts of their village to *Ama* Kuwamo's house. *Ama* Kuwamo was an unmarried mother of a three year-old son, and a close and friendly neighbour of theirs. She had requested them to transport the very firewood that the very men had cut down for her about two months earlier from the forest to her house for three meals a day and as much *ara* and *bangchang* as they could drink. Normally, beside what she was offering for their work, it was customary that she repays their labour with the same number of man-days of work to each of them. However, they had readily accepted her request since she had no man by her side to help her. Nevertheless, the countless heavy loads of firewood that they had carried during the last two days had battered their bodies. So, now that the two days' hard labour was over, they were sited in her small smoky and sooth-ridden kitchen for a customary few rounds of *ara* and a modest dinner. Of course, the hostess knew exactly what would soothe their aching bodies. So, she served them with 'nose cracking' strong *ara* that she had distilled specially for the night from the malt that had been fermented for more than four months. As *Ama* Kuwamo served them the fifth round, she repeated her chorus courtesy for the eleventh time, "Please have some more. This *ara* was distilled from the malt that was fermented for more than eight months." And the malt from which the *ara* was distilled kept growing older with every additional cup of *ara* she helped herself to.

Then, just as the hostess was preparing to serve them dinner, Dolma's breathless face appeared in the doorway. "Tshering, please come home quickly. Tenzin's condition has become quite bad," reported Tshering's wife. Tenzin, their fourth and only surviving child had been complaining of a stomach-ache since five days back, and he had been bedridden for the last two days. Initially, Tshering and his wife had been just anticipating the cause of Tenzin's sickness to be some kind of weather or food related illness that would go away in a flash. But as their son's condition kept on deteriorating, their suspicion of the worst had grown, and they had been waiting for shaman Pema's return to consult him. Unfortunately, Pema was away at a far off village performing rituals for a number of families.

Tshering instantly picked up his cup of *ara*, emptied the cup with one big gulp, licked the inside of the cup clean of *ara,* put the cup in the front pouch of his garment and got up to leave. "Looks like I must take leave, friends," he excused himself.

"But, the dinner! You must eat something before leaving," the hostess objected with genuine concern that none of the five men who had worked so hard to make sure that she has enough firewood for an entire year should go back home without dinner at her place. "And, Dolma, please join us," she invited courteously. "I will serve the two of you right away."

"We must leave immediately," said the couple in unison, and hurried out of the house.

"Please, do come back later," called *Ama* Kuwamo after the couple. "I am sure that Tenzin will be alright."

When Tshering reached home gasping for air, he found his son rolling and wriggling in bed like a cat that had been run over by a bullock cart. As his wife frantically tried to prepare a ritual to appease the evil spirits to free her son, Tshering noticed the colour of his son's body change from a feverish red to a rotting bluish green. And his worst suspicion was confirmed as his child breathed his last and the bluish green patches appeared all over the corpse within seconds. His ex-lover has claimed the life of yet another child of his! He sat there motionless as if in deep meditation holding his dead son in his lap. His eyes were fixed on his wife who was beating her chest with both fists and crying out, "*Kencho sum*, why did you have to take away my only son! You could have taken me instead," again and again. Then, Tshering pressed the palm of his right hand firmly against his heart, looked up at the ceiling with wide opened eyes, and slumped facedown on the dead boy, and lay still.

After a while, when Dolma noticed her husband lying motionless atop their dead son, she held him by his shoulders and shook him up. "Tshering, get up now. He is gone anyway. We must prepare for his last rites," she said in-between sobs desperately trying to console her husband. But her husband did not move at all. So, as she shook him up even harder, he rolled over and lay breathless beside the dead boy. Tshering was also no more. He had not been able to overcome the shock from the death of his fourth and only child. Dolma screamed pathetically time and again shaking up Tshering's senseless body by thrusting him backward and forward with all her force by holding on to his shoulders. One instant she was begging of him not to leave her alone and then on the other she was cursing him for leaving her alone to face the tragedy.

As Dolma's wretched screams reached the ears of her neighbours, more than a dozen neighbours rushed to her rescue. Within a few minutes of their arrival, Dolma's house resembled a scene of the aftermath of a fierce battle on a battlefield, except that there were only two dead bodies and no one was physically wounded. Most of the villagers were shocked by Tshering's sudden death while feeling sorry for Tenzin and Dolma. There were only three elderly men who were trying hard to console Dolma. The rest of the visitors were nothing but streamlets of tears and desperados of cries and sobs. The three elderly men tried to move Dolma away from the ghastly sight. But the widow clung onto her husband's dead body and would not budge. Suddenly, she stopped crying altogether, and lay still too.

The next day, almost every men and women of the village as well as those from the nearby villages were on a long procession to the cremation ground with three corpses wrapped in white cotton cloth. And from a distance, Lhamo was watching the procession, her eyes filled with tears. It had not been her will to let that happen to Tshering. Not her Tshering. She had just wanted her revenge but not his death. She had loved him all those years.

At fifteen, Seldon was the loveliest teenage girl in her village. Her eyes were as bright and tantalizing as the evening star. Her perfectly framed mouth had equally perfect lips that were as red as the petals of a newly bloomed rose flower. Her cheeks that were faintly hued with red seemed to glow with her fair complexion. A cascade of black silky hair flowed down her well proportioned head to her shoulders. Even *Tsari Yuma* would have been jealous of her body that was perfectly proportioned. She walked with the gait of a lioness and spoke with the voice of a nightingale. Wherever she went, boys of her age and those much younger than her, men of all ages with or without wives, and even girls and women of all shapes and sizes all had their eyes on her. She was every lusty man's sexual fantasy, every lover boy's angel, every parent's dream child and every girl's unfulfilled wish. She was indeed like a *Khandoma* reborn on mother earth.

Seldon was loved by her foster parents and their children and admired by all the village folks. Yes, she had all the reasons to live happily. She had all the reasons to dream of a prince from a far off land to pass by her village someday and lift her off her feet, put her on his pony and take her away to his lovely palace to live with him happily ever after. However, everybody, except her foster parents and their children, shied away from her, although with a heavy heart, at the thought of who her blood mother was. Her inborn and physical beauty could not shield her against the shadows cast upon her life by the curse her blood mother had inherited from her ancestors. Although there was no poof, as yet, that she had inherited the curse, people did not forget that she was the destined one. People would never forget that she was the destined one. When she was younger, every now and then a playmate or two would call her a Poison Giver's daughter. She would neither complain nor try to defend herself, but would always run away to a lonely place and cry alone till her eyes ran out of tears and she could cry no more. Then, she would run to her foster parents and ask them if there was any way she could get away from the intolerable insult. Initially, they had tried to defend her by either spanking the 'big mouths' or threatening to give them a nice spanking if they ever called Seldon a Poison Giver's daughter. However, with time even they had grown tired of defending her and had resorted to telling her that time would put everything in place, and that she must be patient. She had been patient for all those years.

Seldon's mother never came to see her and Seldon was not permitted to visit her either. Of course, that did not matter much when she was a child. However, as she grew older, she realised that the couple she had taken to be her parents were not really her biological parents. This would often build up a very strong longing for her parents deep down in her heart that would make her miss her parents terribly, and she would often feel a strong urge to go and meet her mother. The first and the last time she had ever seen her mother in person was during a *Wang* ceremony in another village when she was twelve. She had seen a tall lady looking at her time and again but avoiding eye contact with her every time she looked at her. Then, an elderly woman sitting beside her had told her that the tall lady was actually her biological mother. When her foster father who was also sitting beside her had heard the lady, he had shouted at her and told her to mind her own business. Then, when she looked towards the crowd where her mother had been standing moments ago, she had seen her hurrying away and disappearing into the crowd. Since then, the very scene would haunt her quite often. But she had never made an attempt to visit her since her foster parents forbade her. Nevertheless, when she was fifteen, her foster parents had one day sent their children away, locked the door behind, and told her most of the things she was supposed to know about her ancestors.

Beside what is already known to the reader, Seldon's foster father Dhendup was her mother's only surviving illegitimate half brother. By the time Lhamo was about to give birth to Seldon, she had realised that she had already inherited the curse. Lhamo had then approached Dhendup with a secret mission. She had confided in him about her having already inherited the curse, and virtually begged him to adopt Seldon. She had even promised him that she would neither see Seldon nor touch her after Seldon was born. She had also promised never to visit his village as long as she lived. Besides, she had made Dhendup promise her never to let Seldon know who her biological parents were or anything about her family until Seldon was of marriageable age.

"My mother and grandmother had kept the curse a secret from me till the time it was too late for me to make a change in my life. I have hope that my child will be spared of the curse till she is of marriageable age and or if she is brought up beyond the shadows of the four pillars of our cursed home. I don't want to forsake her of her right to something as important as taking a decision between being a killer and a life giver. And the only way I can give her the right is by not letting the curse take her over before she had the chance to make a choice. I have hope that the curse will not touch her as long as someone, other than my mother or myself, brings her up, and as long as she is forfeited of all of my family's material inheritances," Lhamo had explained when Dhendup had asked why she was doing that. "And who better than you, my brother? Who better than you? Please, have mercy on my child and rescue her from this bondage," she had pleaded with folded hands, tears streaming down her face.

"Please, stop crying and go home in peace, my sister. I will do as you wish," Dhendup had consented. "But you must keep your part of the promises as well," he had cautioned his half-sister.

"I will, brother," Lhamo had promised. "But one thing more! I also don't want to deprive her of her rich inheritance that our ancestors had painstakingly accumulated over scores of years. So, please tell her everything when she is old enough to understand and take the right decision. Should she decide to give up the curse and therefore all her inheritance, I will die a happy person. But should she decide to come home and claim her inheritance and take upon herself the curse, woe shall be mine, my dear brother," Lhamo had declared.

"I understand your pains, sister. My wife and I will not let you or our child down," he had promised his half-sister weeping uncontrollably as his heart melted like a piece of butter on a hot pan out of sympathy for her.

"We will bring up your child like one of our own, sister," Dhendup's wife had assured her as well.

Just as Lhamo had started to feel the labour pains, she had sent a cow herder to inform Dhendup and his wife about the delivery of her child. On hearing the news, Dhendup's wife had hurriedly fried three brown eggs and some garlic in butter, and packed it neatly in a wooden bowl with lid. Then, she had also heated some *ara* in fried eggs, and poured it into a *palang,* and the couple had hurried to Lhamo's rescue. Seldon had been born in a cowshed at a distance from her Lhamo's house within minutes of their arrival. When Dhendup's wife picked up the infant, Lhamo had told her to take the child away immediately, and to leave her alone. At that moment, she had passed the child to her husband, and served Lhamo with the *ara* and the fried eggs, against Lhamo's will, so that Lhamo could regain her energies. Afterall, that was a customary thing to do. Then, her foster mother who was breast-feeding her own three-month old daughter had breast-fed Seldon, and taken her home. Ever since, her uncle and aunt like their own daughter had brought up Seldon.

"You are only fifteen, and not yet old enough to digest the truth, Seldon. However, we have no choice but to tell you everything at this stage," her uncle said, tears rolling down his cheeks, while her aunt lay by her side holding her hand and sobbing quietly.

"I can handle the truth, *apa*. I can handle it, especially now that I am aware of the pains you all had taken for me all these years. I can handle the truth, *apa*. Please tell me everything," Seldon pleaded as the salty tears that rolled down her red eyes started to drench the front of her blouse.

"We could have waited longer to tell you everything, but we decided against it since..." he tailed off.

"Since what, *apa*?" demanded Seldon.

"Late Tenzin was your biological father, Seldon. We had also kept this a secret from you all these years," he unfolded another truth as lightly as possible.

"You mean that man in Shamling who has died of a heart attack at his son's death?" she inquired, shock written all over her face.

"Yes. People say that he had died of a heart attack when he realised that his son had died of poison," he said looking away. "Like his other children," he added with a deep sigh.

"*Lama kheno!* Why so?" Seldon broke down again as the unspeakable truth spoke for itself.

"Tomorrow is his 21st day rites, and we were wondering if you would like to pay your last respects to him!" said her uncle.

Early next morning Seldon accompanied her uncle and aunt went to her father and his family's last rites. When they were about to enter the monastery where the rites were being performed, an old lady waylaid Seldon. "You Poison Giver! Your mother has killed my son, my daughter in-law and all my grand children. Now are you here to kill the rest of us?" the old lady screamed with fury.

"*Aie*, my daughter is here to pay her last respects to her father. I understand that your family is going through a rough time, and I sympathise. But please control yourself, and don't insult my daughter in a public place like this," her uncle reasoned.

"Your daughter? Do you think that by addressing this witch as your daughter you can change her destiny? She will soon be no better than her mother," the old lady shouted. "She will be nothing more than a Poison Giver, and you and I and everybody knows it," she continued to scream attracting all the guests to the spot.

"Stop this nonsense or else," her uncle warned with his right hand on the handle of his dragger, fuming with rage.

Seldon and her aunt quickly grabbed him, and pleaded him to leave the monastery. As they walked away, the old lady spat at Seldon and screamed after her repeatedly till they were way out of sight. A helpless Seldon tried to cry her shame away as the trio headed towards their village. After Seldon stopped crying, her uncle said, "It was all my fault. I should have known better than to suggest you to attend your father's 21st day rites, Seldon," repenting his own virtue.

"It is not your fault, *apa*," Seldon consoled her foster father. "I am only glad that we have at least tried to pay our respects to..." and she broke down again.

That night after the rest of the family had gone to sleep, Seldon approached her uncle and aunt. "*Apa* and *ama*, I have taken my decision," she announced in a low murmur. Her uncle and aunt exchanged a nervous glance at each other and looked at her. After a long silence that seemed like eternity, her uncle asked in a low quivering voice what her decision was, his shaking hands holding hers softly.

"All these years, I have tried to swallow the bitter gall quietly," she said carefully. "People have always tried to avoid me, and my playmates have called me a Poison Giver time and again. And today...." She sobbed leaning on her uncle's shoulder. "I have had enough, *apa*! I have had enough!"

"Seldon, you must not feel this way. You know that what people call you is not true, and..." her aunt tried to console her.

"No, *ama*, I have had enough. No matter what, I will always be a Poison Giver or a Poison Giver's daughter all my life," Seldon interrupted her aunt.

"Please, don't say such horrible things, *bomey*," pleaded her aunt.

"I understand how much it must hurt you, Seldon. But this is no way to deal with it," advised her uncle.

"So, I have decided to leave this village and all of you. I will go away to a far off place where nobody would know me, and start my life anew," Seldon declared as if she has not heard a word her uncle and aunt had said.

"But you are just a girl of fifteen! How can we let you leave your home!" exclaimed her uncle who was taken aback totally.

"No, Seldon, please don't say such a thing. Please don't leave us. How can you leave us all? How have we deserved this?" complained her foster mother.

"Please try to understand me, *ama*. I love and respect you all a lot, but this is what I must do. I have no choice," declared Seldon.

"But you are only fifteen, Seldon!" emphasised her uncle. "How can we let you go away to a far off place alone!" insisted Dhendup. "*Aye*, if only I had not promised my sister that I will let you take the decision after I have told you the truth!" regretted her uncle.

"I must or I will never be able to live in peace ever again in my life," reasoned Seldon.

"If you must really leave, I am coming with you," said a voice from the dark corner of the room taking the trio by surprise. It was Wangchuk, her nineteen-year old cousin.

"What are you doing in the dark like a ghost? Come out her," commanded his father.

"And what are you three doing in the middle of the night discussing such an important issue all by yourselves?" accused the young man. "I knew something was fishy when the three of you didn't go to bed," continued Wangchuk as he sat down beside Seldon. The trio was lost for words. "And how dare you try to run away from me, ha! Did I not beat up all those village kids who had dared to call you names? Besides, did I not love you more than I loved my brothers and sisters? How dare you!" accused Wangchuk, giving her a soft punch on her shoulder as his tears entered his mouth leaving its saline taste lingering in his mouth. "I will accompany you even to hell if you wish to go there," he announced as she embraced him crying.

The four remained sobbing in the quietness of the dark for a long time. Then, Dhendup broke the silence. "Alright, now that Wangchuk has agreed to accompany Seldon, I know that we don't have to worry much about her safety," Dhendup said turning to his wife. The, turning to Seldon and Wangchuk he declared, "So, we will prepare for your departure tomorrow. And you can leave at the cock's third crow early day after tomorrow," and unfolded his plan, "We will load everything you need on to four ponies. But do not leak out the secret. Not even to your brothers and sisters," cautioned Dhendup. Then, after a long pause he continued in a sad tone, "But, Seldon, you must promise us that you will come to see us before we die of old age. And Wangchuk you must promise us that you will be good to her and that you will protect her even if it should cost you your own life."

"I promise," said the two eagerly almost in unison.

Lhamo sang melancholy as she picked up dried pinecones and tossed them into the large bamboo basket on her back. Her heart breaking song sang in the melancholy of her beautiful voice could have sent a cuckoo into hiding with shame. The songs filled the pine forest and echoed back from the distant rocky cliffs. Then, she stopped abruptly and said, "Just a few more basket full will do the job," as she walked towards her house carrying the bamboo basket full of pinecones.

Well, Lhamo has been collecting dry pinecones for the last two days. She has already filled up the large empty space in the ground floor of her house, where she and her mother stored the grains, with the pinecones.

She has also pilled up the attic with hay, straw and pinecones. "Something tells me that we are going to have a very cold winter this year, *ama*." she had replied when her mother had asked her that morning why she was collecting so much of dry pinecones.

"But we have enough firewood to last for more than a year," her old mother had reminded her.

"No harm having a little more," she had tried to convince her mother.

"But storing them under the house as well as on the attic could be dangerous," her mother had cautioned her.

"Are you afraid of a fire disaster, *ama*?" she had teased her mother. "But why should you, *ama*? The cauldron will protect you, won't it?" she had added as if trying to make fun of the old lady.

"All right, what ever you say, Lhamo!" her mother had given up the argument, and she had kept on collecting the cones and filling up the empty spaces in her house.

As Lhamo walked towards her house, she recalled her brother Dhendup's visit two days ago. He had called her from a distance from her house, and when she ran up to him too eager to find out why her half brother wanted to meet her, he had announced, "Lhamo, I have fulfilled my part of the promise that I made to you fifteen years ago." And he had told her everything including how Seldon's paternal grandmother had insulted her at her father's last rites, and that Wangchuk and Seldon had left the village for an unknown destination five days ago. "I hope that you will be happy, now that Seldon has taken the right decision," he had summed up his visit. And that had been the best news she had ever heard in her whole life. And she had shed tears of joy for the first time in her life.

"Brother, I don't know how to thank you, but I promise you that I will do something Seldon will be proud of someday," she had promised her brother.

"I have just fulfilled my promise to you, and my duty as Seldon's foster parent. You be a good woman now," Dhendup had advised her and walked away.

That evening when she walked into the altar room, her mother was standing in the middle of the room holding the cauldron in both her hands and staring at it. "Anything wrong, *ama*?" she asked casually.

"Can't you hear the noise, and can't you see it moving?" said her mother terrified lifting the cauldron to her face.

"No, *ama*" she lied terrifying the old lady even more, although she could see and hear whatever her mother saw and heard. In fact, she had been hearing the clanking noises of the silver coins in the cauldron since the day Dhendup had paid her a visit, and she knew exactly why.

"This is a bad omen for me!" gasped her mother, believing that she is the only one who sees what she sees and hears what she hears.

"Stop this nonsense, *ama!* I am sick and tired of this stupid cauldron!" Lhamo yelled. She grabbed the cauldron from her mother, flung it into a corner, and stormed out of the room. And while she was sitting in the kitchen, she could hear the clanking noise growing even louder.

That night after her mother had gone to bed in the altar room, she sat in the kitchen alone murmuring a prayer. At around midnight, she securely locked the altar room from the outside. Then, she quietly spread all her cloths and mattresses on the floor in her room that was adjacent to the alter room. She walked quietly to the kitchen, took a bundle of pine-wood flint in both hands, lit one, and quietly ran out of the kitchen to the room in the ground floor. She carefully laid the bunch of burning flint under the dry cones. When the fire started to spread in the room, she lit up the other bunch of flint, ran upstairs to the attic, and set fire there. Then, she fumbled her way down the stairs and took the basket full of cones which she had put outside the kitchen door during the day, latched the kitchen door behind her securely, and poured half of the cones on to the oven. She quickly put all the firewood near the oven on the cones and a bunch of pine-wood flint splinters into it and set it on fire. Then, she ran to her own room and latched it behind. By then, her room was already filled with smoke and she could already feel the heat of the fire in the ground floor.

"Lhamo, wake up! Our house is on fire," her mother yelled from within coughing her lungs out.

"I know, *ama!* I set it on fire," she yelled back as she lit the rest of the cones she had heaped up against a pile of wooden boxes in her room and set it on fire with a bunch of burning flint.

"You crazy women! Open the door," her mother yelled coughing hard as she tried to force open the door.

"Why don't you tell the cauldron to do it, ha!" she yelled back. Lhamo heard the old lady fumbling at the window desperately trying to open it. "I have already nailed up the windows, *ama*. So don't waste your breath trying to open them," Lhamo yelled as she heard her mother's long nails scratching at the windows. By then, the roof was fully ablaze, and the fire from under the house has already started to flare up the sides of the house and catch the floor.

Her mother was screaming with pains as the fire from the roof and the windows started to creep into the altar room and set everything ablaze. "Lhamo, *kuchey*, let me out of here?" begged her mother screaming.

"Scream, you witch. Scream as much as you can," Lhamo shouted back as her own room was ablaze and the fire was already creeping up her *kira*. "Let me see how the cauldron saves you. You and your mother made me a Poison Giver. You people made me kill a lot of innocent people including my Tshering," she yelled to her screaming mother. "Tonight I will put an end to you and me and the cursed cauldron," she vowed like a woman possessed. And slowly the fire engulfed Lhamo.

The fire was noticed only the next morning by a cow herder who hurriedly informed the residents of a nearby village. As the first group of people reached the site with the hope to help, there was almost nothing left of the house or the house owners, except for the mud baked walls of the house and a heap of red charcoals. The group left the site with a mix feeling of sympathy for the victims and joy at the end of a hierarchy of Poison Givers. As the group reached the top of the hillock that barred their village the view of the place where just hours ago had stood the Poison Givers' family's isolated house, they turned back and took a last look at the smoky remains of the house. The morning sun shone brightly across their heads on the distant ruins. And to their surprise, something in the middle of the ruins glittered brightly in the morning sun. However, no one neither dared nor cared to go back and find out what it was.

Meanwhile, somewhere in a far off valley, Seldon and Wangchuk were happily crossing a bamboo suspension bridge, hand in hand. On the other side of the bridge, a traveller was courteously restraining his black mule as the twosome approached him. "Where are you young couple headed to?" asked the stranger.

"To the land of our dreams, *lopon*," Wangchuk replied smartly while Seldon giggled clinging on to his shoulder. "And where are you headed to, *lopon*?" Wangchuk asked out of courtesy.

"To Shamling and the neighbouring villages," the stranger replied. "Do you come from one of those villages by any chance?" he inquired.

The young couple looked at one another, smiled and shook their heads in unison, "Never heard of the place, *lopon*."

Then, as the stranger looked on, the young couple headed up the valley, with four loaded ponies happily clinging to one another, giggling and laughing, and slowly disappeared from his view. The stranger smiled and nodded to himself as the happy and smiling faces of the young couple lingered on his mind and their laugher and giggles echoed in his ears for a while.

As the lonely stranger neared his destination, he came across a house by the roadside that has been reduced to ashes only days ago. He stood there for a moment and sympathised for the people for their losses although he did not know to whom the house had belonged, and hoped that the disaster had not hurt anyone. Then, something caught his eyes. Something reflected the rays of the evening sun directly into his eyes. And like a man possessed, he slowly made his way towards the glittering object, his hand shielding his eyes against the strong reflection. Then, as his eyes fell on a silver cauldron with beautiful gold carvings and filled to the brim with silver coins, he could not believe his luck. He inspected the surroundings throwing a hasty glance, and quickly grabbed his new-found fortune, ran to his horse and retraced the path that he just came by. With this kind of money, he could buy almost everything he had ever wanted. There was no reason why he should visit the nearby villages in search of new business prospects, not anymore.

***

# *A new legacy for a village*

The full moon shone proudly in a cloudless sapphire sky, while the envious stars beyond twinkled ostentatiously trying to distract an earthling viewer's attention, if any. The night dragged on grudgingly under his radiance. He did not seem to be bothered by the stars' jealousy or the village's stray dogs' purposeless barking. After all, this was his night. Half the world may be in deep slumber but without the clouds obstructing its radiance and the sun long due, the world was for him to shine on. This surely was his night. But not for Zangpo. Zangpo looked at the sky time and again for any sign of moving clouds. At least he did not desire the moon to light up the night thus. He had work to do, and he worked better in the refuge of the darkness of the night.

Zangpo walked casually along the deserted single footpath that ran carelessly through his village of twenty-three households that had the look of a cluster of colonies of termites' nests forged out of brown earth. He stood still, stared at the sky again, shook his head disapprovingly at the moon and scratched his head. Then, like a busy banker late for work he looked at his cheap Indian made Ricoh wristwatch, which he had stolen from a government official who had visited his village a couple of weeks ago. "1:32 a.m.," he sighed. "Just about the right time!" he spoke to himself knowing that everybody in the village would be fast asleep at this hour of the night.

As he neared his workplace for the night, he looked at the sky again. He shook his head again with discontentment. "So what if they woke up and recognised me!" he challenged his conscience. "I can just walk away and they would not even bother to talk to me about it after tonight," he remarked boldly. But then, he stood completely motionless for a while scratched his head and tried to justify the need to urgently execute the errand at hand. "If I don't finish up the job tonight, they are not going to forget about the booty on their roof again. They will just put it all away tomorrow, and I will have to wait for someone else to forget a similar booty outside their house or on the roof. And that doesn't happen everyday," he reasons out with himself. "... I would rather not take the risk of having to break into their house some other day; you never know when someone will lose his patience," he concludes, finally justifying himself to finish up the job he had set out for, although the moon was not being kind enough for him by shining too brightly at the very moment.

Zangpo scanned the house from a block away. His trained eyes could see only a small flickering light in the altar room through the window devoid of a shutter. "That is just a butter lamp," he reassured himself. Then, as he reached outside the house, he tiptoed up the granite steeps to the front door. There he placed his ear against the door, stopped his breath and tried to pick up any discernible sound coming from within the house. He could hear only the noisy snores of a fast asleep old man. Then, suddenly he heard a woman's cry coming from within the house, "I said not the aluminium pot!"

"That's only old Peldonmo talking in her sleep. She always talks in her sleep!" Zangpo convinces himself. And he could not help but wonder as to why some people talk in their sleep. He tiptoed backwards being cautious not to let the old borer infested wooden floor under his feet creak and also not to dump into the bronze cauldron of water that there.

Once at a safe distance from the front door of the house, he scratched his head again and remembered aloud, "I think that I saw the wooden ladder near the cowshed this evening!" Instantly he hurried towards the cowshed that was only about fifty meters away from the house. And loo, there it was. It would surely make the climb easier for him. He put the wooden ladder onto his shoulder and carried it to the rear of the altar room. He knew that nobody would be sleeping in that room that night since the old couple's son and daughter in-law were still in Babtong, a village by the banks of Khomachu river. After he had laid the tip of the ladder smoothly on the shingles of the roof, he pressed down onto the ladder with both hands, slowly increasing the force by exerting the full weight of his body onto it. "Not a sound! Good. Both the shingles and the ladder are strong enough," he chuckled. Then, he threw a casual glance around him to make sure that he did not have any company, and made his way to the rooftop.

Once on the roof, Zangpo looked at the sky again, but with a broad smile this time. It did not matter if the sky did not favour him tonight. After all, there he was right beside his booty. His booty was spread over the shingles, covering almost half of the entire roof of the house. As he took a closer look at his booty, his eyes bulged so far out of their sockets and his mouth opened so wide that had there been a woodpecker hovering around at that very moment, it would have mistaken his mouth for its nest and flown into it. "On such a moonlit night, even a colour-blind man will have no problem

Zangpo makes away with his booty

distinguishing crispy sun-dried beef from brown dry creepers," he remarked with exalted anticipation of his fortune. "Quality beef from a pregnant Mithun crossbred cow!" he concluded as his chest heaved with excitement. The old couple's Mithun crossbred cow had died the day before after having fallen over a cliff while foraging in the forest. "And the whole lot of it too!" chuckled Zangpo.

He quickly took out a worn out gunny bag from the front pouch of his garment and started to fill it up. Although the excitement was clear in the twinkles of his wide opened eyes, he moved across the roof as swiftly as an eagle on hunt pouncing on a chick and quieter than a mischievous cat in a miserly landlord's rations storeroom.

"Almost half of it all already. That's it. One can't be too greedy! So, I must leave some for the host as well," he murmured to himself. Nevertheless, just as he was about to fling the sack of the booty over his shoulder and rush back home, his eyes rested on a heap of bones on the far end of the roof. "Well, I better take some of those too. They make good soup and go well with potatoes and pumpkins as well," he decided.

"Where have you been, Zangpo? You are as cold as a rock?" inquired his wife as he got into the blanket beside her.

"Cook some large pieces of dry beef for lunch. I think we have not eaten meat for a while now," he said calmly with a clear tone of satisfaction in his voice. "Now, we have enough to last for more than three months," he assured his wife. "Since it is well dried, I have put it in the rice box downstairs."

"I hope nobody saw you!" wished Choikimo.

"Don't speak like a fool. Just who walks around the village at this time of the night!" he assured his wife. "Except me and the ghosts!" he added.

"Did we forget the meat on the roof last night?" inquired old Peldonmo of her husband over a breakfast of maize powder pudding, salted dry red chilli salad enriched with fermented cheese and salted butter tea.

"I think we did," replied her husband as a matter of fact.

"I'll go pack them up before the crows and the stray cats get them," she volunteered and hurried out of the kitchen, leaving her half eaten breakfast behind.

"Can't we finish the breakfast first!" grumbled the old man after her.

After a while, *"Maymay! Wai, maymay!"* called the old lady after a while. "Did you leave the ladder pinned to the roof yesterday? How could you! You sure did help the cats get to the meat with ease, didn't you!" she complained.

"I did not. I remember putting it away." He scratched his head trying to make sure. "Yes, I used it to get down some hay from the roof of the cowshed, and I did put it there near the cowshed," explained her husband at the top of her voice as he rushed out of the house to calm her down.

"Than why is it be here?" grumbled the wife as she climbed up the ladder.

"How did...?" He scratched his silver haired head again trying to figure out how it had gotten there.

"*Maymay!* Come up here and look at what is left of our meat!" yelled the old lady from the roof.

The old man dutifully hurried up the ladder to the roof. He preferred not to flare up his wife, at least not at the start of a new day. If he did, she would scream at him and everyone else in the village for the rest of the day.

"Just look at this. Where is the rest of the meat gone?" she fumed with anger accusing her old husband of the misfortune.

"May be they look less because they have dried up. And...and, may be the cats and the crows got some as well, but I am sure that they did not take away too much either," fumbled the old man helplessly.

"Do you mean to tell me that cats and crows can eat up or take away half a cow's meat? Don't you tell me that they were working as a team and took away all those bones too!" yelled the wife. "Can't you see that someone has stolen our meat?" And before the old man could figure out what to say next, she continued, "I know who stole our meat. Zangpo did it. Who else but Zangpo would do such a thing? Yes, Zangpo stole them last night."

"Calm down now! I am sure nobody stole anything. And don't point fingers at somebody without any proof," cautioned the old man.

"Who else would steal meat from someone else's roof in this village, if not Zangpo? He is the only person who would do such a thing in this village," she screamed back at him as if she had full confidence in her accusation.

"I said calm down, Peldonmo!" commanded her husband in a cold voice that could have made even a warlord tremble with fear. "It is not right to point fingers at someone without any concrete proof of a misdeed," he advised her again.

"But...but even you know that he did it, don't you?" tried to persuade the lady sheepishly in a murmur.

"Just let it be, alright!" commanded the man sternly. "If someone has stolen our meat, you can bet that the person had a good reason to. After all, he's got to feed his family too," reasoned the old man compassionately.

"But he could have just asked for it, and we would have given him some. Why should he steal from an old couple!" lamented the old lady.

"Let's just go back in and finish our breakfast before it gets cold," said the old man in a godly voice after helping his wife to pack up what was left of their meat.

A few days later, Thinlay, the lay monk caretaker of the village's monastery, was on his way to fetch water from the village's only water source, a small stream about two kilometres away from the village on which the village folks depended for their drinking water. As usual, he was already half way to the stream by the fifth crow of the rooster. After all, he must get the first serving of the water of the day from the stream for the monastery. This necessitated him to be the first person of the village to get to the stream. As he was passing through a dark thicket of giant wild ferns, he saw a dark figure carrying something heavy on his back approaching him. He stood frozen, his heart trying to beat out of his chest as he anticipated the unimaginable. As he fumbled for a prayer, the silhouette approached him nearer and nearer. And, just as he was about to scream and draw his dragger, he recognised the figure. It was Zangpo in his black cotton garment carrying a load of firewood. "*Wai,* Zangpo, why are you up so early? You almost frightened the soul out of me!" commented Thinlay.

"Oh, it is you, *lopon koenyer!* I thought I will start the day a little early today," replied Zangpo casually. "So you are on your way to get water for the offering?" asked Zangpo out of courtesy.

"Yes. You should not work too hard, Zangpo!" said Thinlay blankly.

"I don't have much choice, do I? Got a wife and three kids to support," replied Zangpo as if trying to justify his conduct.

"I guess you are right!" agreed Thinlay without a second thought.

"I will be on my way now. You be careful, *lopon koenyer*. I heard a leopard's cry just a few minutes ago. It may not come this way, but you never know," he cautioned Thinlay and continued towards the village.

"Stealing other's firewood!" Thinlay passed a solitary remark as he walked towards the stream. "So it is true that Zangpo steals others' firewood that has been left in the forest to dry! How shameless of him! Start work early today indeed! Stealing other's firewood! How disgusting!" repented pious Thinlay. He knew that the firewood Zangpo was stealing belonged to Ugyen Dorji, a close neighbour, because he was the only man who had chopped firewood in the forest nearby the village's drinking water source. In fact, Ugyen had hired ten men from the village for a day to fell half a dozen oak trees and chop them up about a week ago. He was also aware of the fact that Zangpo was used to stealing the village folks' firewood. He had heard numerous rumours about it, besides others.

While Thinlay was filling up his kettle with fresh water from the stream, his subtle mind was full of concern about Zangpo's misconduct in the village. He knew that Zangpo was going too far with his stealing and burglary habits. He felt that Zangpo was taking advantage of the village residents' understanding and goodwill. The villagers would neither accuse Zangpo directly into his face of stealing nor would they report against him to the authorities. "I hope that he understands that people don't do these in goodwill towards his wife's relatives and not because of himself," wishes Thinlay. "Some day people may stop putting up with his behaviour, and that might as well be his end," he reasons to himself. "Or may be not! People in this village are too religious to harm even a fly," he contradicts his own logic. "No wonder he never went away from this village since the time he first settled down here after getting married to Choikimo. If anybody is reaping the fruits of compassion in this village, it is Zangpo! He will surely be remembered, long after he is gone, as the first, if not the last, professional thief of Goenpakap."

About a week later, Dawamo a fifty three-year old widow was busy with seventeen other hired hands harvesting potatoes. She could hardly hide her smiles of self-contentment at the size and numbers of tubers each plant yielded. Every time the man in front of her spaded an old wrinkled and either decaying or drying plant, her eyes rolled with excitement at her own fortune. It was a good year. And she still had her field of corn in which each plant carried at least two large ears packed with large evenly sized yellow grains, to look forward to. Yes, provided that the monkeys, bears, wild boars and barking deer did not claim their share before the harvest. But she was confident that her son would not let them since he guards the field day in and day out.

"Such large potatoes! And just look at the number of tubers under each plant!" exclaimed the man in front of her. "Did you use cow dung to make the soil fertile, *Ama* Dawamo?

"No, I did not. I must say that the Goddess of the fields is kind to the widow," remarked Dawamo piously.

"You are a lucky woman!" complemented the man.

Dawamo hardly heeded the complement. She was lost in her own thoughts. At the back of her head she was already planning as what to do with her bumper harvest. She was already making up her mind that she would put away some potatoes to be used as seeds for next year, and than take about twenty horse loads to Phagidung, Babtong and Khoma to barter with rice. She spared a secret smile of self-contentment again as she picked up the freshly unearthed tubers and filled the large bamboo basket beside her. Secretly, she calculated that fifteen to twenty baskets would suffice her home needs. "Yes, I'll still have a few baskets to give away to Choiney, Damcho and Penjor. They didn't plant potatoes this year. And of course, to Kezang! She gave me a lot of her delicious peaches and..." she spoke aloud unconsciously.

"*Ama* Dawamo, your store is almost full. If we dump any more potatoes there, you will hardly have enough space to move around the rice box. Where do you want us to store the rest of the potatoes?" asked her neighbour's daughter. Dawamo had hired the girl as one of the seven girls to help her transport the harvest from the field to her house while the men dug up the potatoes. Dawamo always stored her potatoes in the spacious store, on the ground floor of her two-storied house. She would always secure the room with a large brass lock minted on her request five years ago by a Tibetan blacksmith who visited her village once every two years.

"Full already!" exclaimed Dawamo. "Good thinking, Sonam. We will store the rest on the attic," she added. Then, she sat down carelessly on the freshly unearthed soil with her back against the basket of potatoes, slipped the strap of the basket onto her head and stood up with the basket on her back as Sonam slightly lifted the basket with both her hands and gave it a slight push to help the lady get up with ease. "I will go ahead and put up a strong ladder to the attic. I don't want my old ladder to break down under your weights and hurt you young ladies," she giggled like an eight year-old girl. As she walked through the middle of the field she called out, "Every one, please don't forget to put aside some good ones for yourselves to take home later."

"*Aaa*, that is not necessary, *Ama* Dawamo!" murmured some workers, more out of courtesy than anything else.

"*Aaa*, please do take some, even if it is just enough for a meal or two," she insisted keeping up with the tradition of insisting someone to accept an offer which will eventually be accepted by the other party after repeated insistence.

It was well past midnight, but Dawamo lay wide-awake in her bed. Her bones, and her back in particular, ached from the hardship of the day's work. She knew that she must get a good night's sleep since she had still got to get up early the next morning and cook her breakfast and milk her two cows. But then, her mind kept wondering around. "I must stop thinking about anything now! I must. I must try to get some sleep," she decided.

She tossed and turned around and shut her eyes tight and tried to go to sleep. After a long last she felt her eyes become drowsy, and she floated off happily into a deep slumber as the sleep worked its balm on her aching body. Then, suddenly she woke up to a creaking sound from the ceiling. She listened intently through the darkness of the room. A thud! Another thud, and yet another one. "There is something or somebody in my attic! What could it be?" she wondered, her heart beating at an uncontrollable pace. "Some troubled soul wandering in my attic in the middle of the night!" guessed her timid mind without a second thought. As her body shivered at the thought, she pulled the blanket over her head, and tried not to get distracted by the sounds from the attic. But in vain. She only grew more tensed and began to concentrate on the sounds even more. "Could it be a ghost? How I wish my son were here!" She felt the hairs on her body rise. "No. No, it can't. There are no ghosts in my house. No reason to be," she consoled herself.

As the noise on the attic continued, she pulled the blanket off her face and listened carefully again. As the thudding noises continued almost rhythmically, she heard the sound of her potatoes rolling on the ceiling. Then, some dry soil fell on her face from the crevices in the ceiling. "There is someone in the attic. A thief! Yes, it must be Zangpo. He is stealing my potatoes," she guessed. *"Ayee*, why should he take the trouble of stealing some potatoes in the middle of the night when all he has to do is ask me for some," thought Dawamo with a mix feeling of disgust and sympathy for the man.

She tried to go back to sleep again but the sounds from her attic would not give her the pleasure. "This man will never change! Why can't he ask people for what he wants from them?" she wondered. Then, after a while, "Of course, he is too shy to ask for any favour from others. He is a very shy man, this Zangpo," she convinced herself. "But stealing is worst than even begging while seeking favours from others is a way of life for many," she contradicted herself as her moral logic took over.

Then, she realised the thudding noises were the results of Zangpo hurriedly filling up his bamboo basket with her potatoes. "Well who else, but him!" she exclaimed. "That is alright. Let him take some. It's enough that I know who is stealing my potatoes. So, I won't even give him the pleasure of letting him know that I am aware of his presence in my attic," she decided with a pretext. "You never know what an ashamed man would be capable of doing to someone who brings the shame upon him," she thought finally accepting the fact.

After a while that seemed like eternity to Dawamo, she heard Zangpo climb down the ladder that was laid against the attic from the kitchen room where she was sleeping. When she peeped from beneath her blanket, she was both amazed and amused by the sight. Zangpo casually descended the ladder with a big bamboo basket on his back, unlatched the door, opened the door, walked out and closed the door behind. Dawamo wondered as to how Zangpo had gotten into her attic and why she had not heard anything at all when he got on to the attic. "He is really good at what he does," she accepted. "And he just made away with a bamboo basket full of my potatoes." She almost laughed aloud. "And he doesn't even have a clue that I know everything about it!" She giggled as she tried hard not to laugh aloud at Zangpo's ignorance of not knowing that she was wide-awake. However, for a man of Zangpo's calibre, it would have been hard for anyone to judge if he even cared if Dawamo knew about his burglary. At least one can be sure of the fact that Zangpo knew that her son would not be around since he had to sleep in a hut in the middle of a corn field on the outskirts of the village guarding the crops from wild animals. Zangpo also knew that Dawamo would not dare to even open her mouth even if she caught him red handed. She was too timid.

"Ah, I have to latch the door again," Dawamo decided. But she did not move out of the comfort of her bed for a long time. Finally, she decided that since Zangpo has already taken what he wanted, there was no point in trying to latch the door. And she went back to sleep.

After only about an hour of her sleep, Dawamo woke up to the same sounds from the attic again. "What? Am

I dreaming?" she spoke aloud. She listened intently, but she was not mistaken about the recurring incident. "This is too much!" murmured Dawamo fuming with anger. But she was afraid to even breathe properly.

Just then, she heard her visitor make his way to the ladder. Again, she peeped at the dark figure in the darkness of the night from under her blanket. And down the ladder he came and out he went through the front door again with a large bamboo basket full of her potatoes on his back. Just as he disappeared behind the door, she threw the blanket off her and dashed to the door. She slammed the door with all her might. "You greedy stray dog!" she yelled after Zangpo. "You took away two baskets of my potatoes in a single night. How could you do such a shameless thing! Don't you know that I reaped my potatoes with the sweat of my brows!" she screamed. "Taking advantage of a lonely lady! Shame on you, Zangpo."

The walls of her house might have echoed her berating, but immediately after she stopped her helpless reprisal, the night was as quiet and calm as the starry sky. By the time she got back in her bed, the village's lead rooster crowed dutifully announcing the arrival of dawn.

"It's all right," she consoled herself. "He already knows that I know about it. That will do. I won't even tell another soul about it now. What good will it do anyway? Worst, especially if my son finds out about it. No, I won't tell anybody," decided Dawamo, the peace-loving lady.

Zangpo was not much of a man to look at. Not that he was poor and a petty thief or a burglar or a 'Yes-Man' in the hands of his fat lazy wife, but for his physique, carriage and ordeal as a man. He was thin and puny, only half the size of his wife. And walked with his knees almost always rubbing together. He also conversed in a voice so low as if he was afraid that the sky would fall on him if he spoke any louder. His face was almost always full of smiles, and he would walk away even from a small boy picking a fight on him. But no village folks could disagree less either that he was also one of the most talented man in the village. No, not for what you already know of him. His hands were as good as gold at carpentry and masonry works. However, since they were never bounded by moral ethics wherever they were, they were hardly hired by the village folks. The word around the village was that if someone hired Zangpo's hands, he must also hire someone else to keep an eye on them.

It was most often than not that after working with Zangpo, one has to go home at the end of the day with a heavy heart. Some lost a saw or a tri-square, a hammer, a planner, a chisel, an axe, a butcher's knife or even a pencil or two, while Zangpo went home a richer man. And every time someone lost something while at work with Zangpo, it was almost customary for him to grumble: "It was right here. How can something disappear in front of one's own eyes?" or "Come now, friends, if any one of you have taken it, please return it. That is the only one I have got," or "It is disgusting to work with a thief," or "*Pah*, if a man loses his things at this rate, he is got to be the only hair to the legendary *Tshongpon* Norbu Zangpo" or yet "*Lama*, if I could steal at this rate, would I not become the richest man in the village!" And all such pitiable or sarcastic comments were passed in such sly ways that the commentator's eyes swayed over Zangpo time and again while a supporter or two would either gesture towards a heedless Zangpo or pass equally pathetic or sarcastic remarks. However, no one would ever go to the extent of directly pointing his fingers at Zangpo. Everybody understood that Zangpo was not just an outsider who had married one of the village's women. He was also somebody's son in-law, a brother in-law, an uncle, a nephew, a husband or a father. Bringing shame upon Zangpo meant insulting at least half the residents of Goenpakap and therefore seeking their grievances in return. And no person would take the risk of blocking the flow of the stream of goodwill amongst the village folks in Goenpakap. Not for a knife or a hammer or for some potatoes or dry beef.

Some village folks even took Zangpo's actions as a form of amusement. Samdrup, the old village astrologer for one was always curious to update himself on Zangpo's latest achievement. The village's youngsters always flocked to him as soon as they had any first hand information on Zangpo. Every time someone narrated what he or she had heard of Zangpo's doing, old Samdrup would burst into uncontrollable laughter till his eyes were steaming with tears and his lungs aching for want for air. "He is good, isn't he? I dare say he is good!" he would say, and burst into laughter again. "Just wait till my wife hears this," he would sum up the conversation and walk away laughing in search of his wife who would almost always be either drunk or getting drunk in one of her neighbours' or relatives' house.

They say Samdrup's wife was as amused as her husband at Zangpo's deeds. And why would not they be? They were fascinated by the tales of the adventures of the legendary burglar, *Awue* Zangku of Western Bhutan. They had heard the tales through some of the village's people who had visited Western Bhutan on either pilgrimage or to sell hand-woven garments or to buy horses. But, they had never had a professional thief in their own village as long as they had lived, till Zangpo had walked into their village one fine day and married Choikimo. And of course, they really thought that stealing things like vegetables, firewood, butter or cheese and even buttermilk or roosters and eggs were very funny. The residents of Goenpakap were just not used to such a thing. However, not everyone shared the same feelings. Some village elders were of the view that Zangpo had not only brought shame upon himself, his family, his relatives and his home but also unleashed a shadow of sinful conduct in the village where Buddha's teachings flowed like Kurichu river. And the young able-bodied men of Goenpakap often swore that should Zangpo not improve his moral ethics, they would teach him a lesson or two. But then again, everybody though it wiser to let Zangpo be and let the goodwill reign in the village.

As for Zangpo, he often thanked his lucky stars for marrying him off to Choikimo in a land so distant from his own home. "Home! Would I have remained a thief all my life if I had not stolen from Kiba's house that fateful night!" he would wonder at times.

He was only nineteen when he had started courting Kiba, daughter of a middle class family. One unfortunate night when he was beside Kiba trying hard to make her reciprocate his love, she had told him that no matter what she would never fall for him since he had nothing to offer her. "But I love you with all my heart, and I am fully committed to do everything humanly possible to keep you happy," he had told her with utmost sincerity trying to convince her.

"Look, Zangpo, if love is everything in life, wouldn't the princesses marry poor peasants' sons who have nothing to offer them but their true love?" she had responded bluntly. "What one owns today is his, but what he hopes to or promises to own tomorrow is like trying to visit Lhasa by crossing the northern mountains blindfolded. You have nothing to be inherited from your parents. So, if I should reciprocate your love and marry you, what kind of a life would I be living? And, how can you feed and clothe the children that you father of me? Love alone isn't enough to start a family," she had concluded.

"But, Kiba, I will work hard and see to it that I earn enough for us to live together happily. Besides, I love...,"

"Zangpo, you don't seem to get what I am saying," she had cut him off. "I am a practical woman. Your love and flowery promises alone can't make me feel secured in life. Once and for all, I must emphasise that I can neither fall for you nor marry you," she had said sternly. "Now you must leave me alone, and never come to see me ever again."

He had left Kiba's place feeling utterly lonely and desperate, shamefully demoralised and with a heavy sense of not belonging. He had not been able to sleep a wink or eat a grain of rice for the next two days. Then, finally his moral judgement had been over-powered by his feeling for urgent need of Kiba's subordination. He had stuck on a seemingly brilliant idea to get even with her for insulting him. "If her parents' wealth is the root cause of her pride and her so-called security, I shall see to it that the root cause is removed for good," he had decided, his heart full of want for vengeance.

Thereafter, he had started visiting Kiba's house every night, and had stolen whatever he could lay his hands on. One unfortunate night, he had been caught red handed. He had not been aware that her father had been waiting with five other men from the village to grab him that night. They had turned his house upside down and taken away every single item that he had painstakingly stolen from Kiba's house. And he had been beaten up black and blue not just by those men but also by his own father. Then, he had been thrown out of his own house by his father.

After that incident, he had lived secretly all alone in a dark enormous rocky cave in a forest, about quarter of a day's walk from his village, chewing on his grievances. And for the next six months he had visited his village secretly every now and than either by day or by night, and had burgled into each and every house in the village, except that of his parents'. Eventually his village folks had reported against him to the police as the prime suspect who plundered their homes. When two policemen started searching the nearby villages for him, he had taken some ration and all the money he had, set fire to everything in the cave, and had run away. Since then, he had never set eyes on his family or his village. Ever since he was also never caught stealing although he had travelled the whole length of Lhuntshi, Mongar and Trashigang districts for four years and stolen a few things from almost every village he had been to. Then, finally he had met Choikimo, and had settled down in Goenpakap. But all those years, he had never stolen any religious items like statues, paintings or scriptures nor had he stolen any expensive robes or jewellery or large sums of money. He had always known that he would never get away by stealing such things. He stole only those things that he needed the most. He never stole to get rich. Nevertheless, through the years, stealing had become a part of his very existence, and eventually a means to his living. And he was neither ashamed nor proud of it. It is said that his standing moral of life was that "a man's got to do what he loves to do the most, and what he is best at."

Well, it has been twenty-five years since Zangpo had started a completely new legacy in Goenpakap. A few things have changed since then. A few fruit trees, which were unheard of in the past bear fruits in Goenpakap now. Many faces have changed. More divorces have taken place than marriages. There are much more children than parents. Houses have grown both in size and number, and most of them now have CGI sheet roofing rather than wooden shingles or thatched bamboo mats. There even seems to be more exotic species of cattle than local and Mithun crosses now. Only a few village lay monks now go around for alms. And by God, Zangpo has grown old.

But even tonight, although the frosts are fast covering the barren earth in the chilly moon lit January night, and even when the dogs prefer to mind the warmth of their homes in the corners of either a cowshed or under a pile of planks neatly stacked up in the sun for seasoning, a lonely figure in a faded blue polyester garment is climbing down Karma's window. He lets his grip off the wooden bar on the window, and lands like a feather on the solid ground outside Karma's two-storied house. He looks around. "All clear," he murmurs. He leans over the sack on the ground, swiftly winds up the rope with which he had gently let down the sack onto the ground through Karma's kitchen window, picks up the sack, flings it over his shoulder and walks away swiftly but silently.

"The fools! They sleep like logs even when I steal their pork right from above their very nose. But surely *Apa* Zangpo will be happy when mother cooks the dried pork for lunch." Dorji has taken after his father. And the legacy started by Zangpo about twenty five years ago in Goenpakap continues.

***

# *Wild mushrooms for mother*

Karma walked joyfully towards his village whistling a familiar tune. He paused momentarily, as he tried to make out to which local song the tune that had come to his lips almost automatically really belonged. He knew that he had heard the song on the concluding night of the local *Tshechu* the previous month. He scratched his head trying to refresh his memory, but in nugatory. Then, he waved the idea away with a quick lift of his eyebrows, and continued to trot and whistle the tune again. After all, he was a happy boy today. Not being able to recollect a song has no bearing to his life what so ever, not today.

"Just wait till I get home and give it to my mother," Karma thought to himself with a grin of self-contentment at the corner of his pink-lipped mouth. And both his hands involuntarily heaved up the front pouch of his garment as if to guess the weight of the content. He paused again, and peeped into the pouch. And as he continued totting gaily again, he threw back his head, and spoke out aloud. "Of course, they are there. Where would they go! They can't walk and they can't fly. They are just mushrooms."

Karma's mother loved wild mushrooms. She would cook mushrooms with chilli and cheese. She would cook mushrooms with potatoes and chilli and cheese. She would cook mushrooms with minced dried beef and hot red dried chilli. She would cook mushrooms with chopped dry bones. She could cook mushrooms with anything and everything. The mushroom recipes she prepared were the envy of all the mothers and housewives in the village. And Karma knew it all too well. In fact, he also knew something more. He knew that the only time his mother had three *bangchu*s (circular basket with cover) of rice at a single meal was when there was mushroom recipe in the house. And every time Karma took home some wild mushrooms, and poured them ostentatiously from the front pouch of his garment into a small circular bamboo basket with lid, when his luck that day was down, or into an open circular basket used for clearing grains, if his luck favoured him, his mother could not hide her joy at the sight of it. "*Way ra rang dragta,* Karma," was always her sincere praise for him.

That would make Karma really happy. He sure loved praises! And why wouldn't he? After all not many people praised him often. And, what more? The praise was coming from his mother. "I will bring more tomorrow, *ama*," he would promise.

So, every day while herding cattle in the forest, Karma would hunt for wild mushrooms. Although he was only nine years old, he could easily identify a number of edible wild mushrooms. He could even smell the presence of a group of wild mushrooms from several yards away. And what more, he could also make out almost exactly the prospect of finding mushrooms by a mere glance at the make-up of any site in the forest. He was also a prolific and successful mushroom hunter, as compared to other village boys of his own age. Nevertheless, he would dutifully follow the four noble rules of thumb of a mushroom hunter the wise men in the past had passed down a line of talented mushroom hunters over many years. The first rule was that one must always keep away from a red mushroom unless he knows it's name, and he has eaten it before, and he is still alive after eating it. The second rule said that one must never eat a mushroom without a name. If he must, he should give a name to the mushroom before eating it. Then, he must let someone nearby know the name given to the mushroom by heart. That person must be asked to stay by his side while he eats it and to take note of what happens to him after he has eaten it. The next rule forbids one to pluck any 'baby mushrooms.' Should one break this rule, it is said that the protecting deity of the forest will hide the mushrooms from him the next time he is on a hunt. The last rule cautions a mushroom curry lover not to trust even his best friend with the address of a family of mushrooms in the thick forest. Of course, Karma was not able to bring home mushrooms every day, not especially during the dry seasons. So, sometimes he would bring home either young bamboo shoots or wild onion leaves, edible ferns, wild asparagus, wild pears and berries, which and whatever he could lay his hands on. Once he had even found a fresh and fully intact deer's leg weighing almost 5 Kg, leftovers of a leopard or some wild dogs. That night the family had had a big feast, and he was even spared a thrashing by his stepfather. But that evening, he was bringing home not berries, not asparagus, not nothing. But the season's first harvest of wild mushrooms and his mother's favourite species of all the wild mushrooms too. Yes, Karma surely had a big reason to be happy.

As he was passing Singye's house, which was just a few blocks away from his own, he saw Singye sitting on an old worn-out cowhide, with a heap of freshly cut poles by his side. He was sharpening one pole into a pointed base with a huge silver bladed dragger that hopelessly tried to reflect the dull evening light. He walked past

Singye stealthily like a thief at work in the middle of the night in the very room of the master of the house he was about to loot. His limited experience cautioned Karma that if Singye found out what he had in the front pouch of his garment, he would be obligated into sharing his booty with the elderly man. No, not that Singye would ask him to, but merely because of the fact that Singye had always been nice to him.

Just then, Singye stopped chopping at the pole and threw a slow lethargic glance at him and remarked, " So, you are coming from the cowshed!"

Karma's cowshed was located at a short walk from his village.

"Yes, uncle Singye."

"Did you lose any cattle today?" asked the elderly man with a grin, more to tease him than anything else.

Karma blushed at the thought of his stepfather thrashing him up every time he found out that a cow had sneaked away and deserted the herd and that Karma had not been able to find her. Karma would lose a cow every now and then, and since his stepfather often milked the cows in the mornings, he would almost always find out about the missing cow. And then, Karma would not be spared of a good thrashing even though his stepfather knew all along that either Karma would find the cow or the cow would return to the herd of her own accord within a few hours or days.

"No, uncle Singye, they are all in the shed tonight," replied the young cowherd.

Just then, the two heard familiar noises of crashing earthen pots and slamming doors, followed by an even more familiar woman's cry. As they simultaneously realised that the cacophony of noises and cries came from Karma's house, Karma suddenly felt his heart in his throat.

"Is that mushroom in your pouch?" asked Singye casually returning the dragger to its sheath. And before Karma had a chance to answer, he continued, "Looks like Kunzang will have to cook it for your mother tonight!'

As Karma stood frozen at another loud noise of a slamming door, the elderly man let out a long sigh and shook his heavy head from side to side remorsefully. "Your stepfather is drunk again," remarked Singye as a matter of fact. "I suggest that you stay here," he added.

Karma stood there like a clay statue in the village's monastery, his half-seasoned brain debating between Singye's proposal and his moral commitment to stand by his mother in times of her woes.

"You heard the door! Your mother will be here sooner or later," reasoned Singye with the understanding of a clairvoyant *Lama* trying to persuade the boy.

Another bang followed by a scream.

"*Ama! Ama!* My *ama!*" muttered the boy through a pair of shaking lips. "I must go," he said aloud finally and started to run towards his house.

"Keep away from the devil," cautioned Singye calling out after Karma. "Just bring your mother along and come back here," he advised.

His mother was on her fours, outside the house near the kitchen door, trying to get up on her feet. Her cries could have been heard miles away. As he ran up to her, and tried to help her up, she stopped crying abruptly, and frantically whispered his name again and again. Then, in a futile attempt to hide her dismal condition from him, she turned her face away and tried to wipe the tears and the blood from her face. He held his mother by her shoulders with both hands. "*Ama! Ama*, are you all right?" he inquired in a whisper.

Just then, the crashing noises inside the kitchen resumed with increased intensity. The air around the house was filled with the noise of crashing earthenware, clanking aluminium pots, ringing copper and brass cauldrons and cracking shelves. As Karma tried to help his mother up again and failed, he started trembling all over. He knew that his stepfather would be coming out any time to beat them up. "*Ama*, please get up. He might come out anytime," he pleaded as he embraced her by her waist and tried to lift her up with all his might.

"Karma, I am feeling a little dizzy," his mother fumbled, as the blood from the gash on her head drenched her blouse.

Then, as karma looked around him nervously as if trying to seek help from some invisible rescuer, his eyes fell on a block of chopped firewood beside his mother. He knew that the block of firewood had no reason to be there. His stepfather had hit her, *his mother*, on the head with that cursed block of firewood. His compassion for his mother's dismay and pain twisted the veins around his very heart that had given birth to them suffocating it. He broke down and cried pathetically, his eyes fixed on his mother's blood stained face, desperately calling out "*Ama! Ama!*" time and again.

"Karma, you stray dog! So, you are finally here," roared his stepfather from within, and started towards the kitchen door.

"Run, Karma, run for your life," cried his mother frantically, pushing him away from her with one hand while she pressed the palm of the other on the ground and tried to get up. A moment later, she slumped face down as her husband opened the kitchen door with all his force and rammed it against the wall. The whole house reverberated under the force of the door slamming against the wall.

"No, *ama!* No. I am not running away and leaving you here. Please get up," pleaded Karma as his stepfather lifted him clear off the ground and threw him half way into the kitchen.

"So, you are going to rescue your mother, ha, you bastard," grunted the drunkard as he slammed the door behind him and secured it with a latch.

"Leave my son alone," screamed the mother. "Somebody help! He is going to kill my son! Help! Help!"

"Let me see who is going to come to your rescue, you witch," shouted back her husband as he made his way towards Karma after giving the door a tug to make sure that it has been securely latched.

As his stepfather approached him, Karma tried to back off towards a corner of the room, frantically skidding on his buttocks by pushing his feet and palms against the floor. His terrified eyes were fixed on his assailant. He swallowed hard on the saliva in his mouth repeatedly to moisten his rapidly drying throat. "I didn't do anything wrong, *apa*! I didn't do anything wrong today," he assured the big angry man. "I didn't lose any cows either, *apa*!"

"Shut up! Just shut up your dirty mouth, you son of the devil," screamed the man, and pulled the boy on to his feet by his ear.

"*Kuchey, apa!* Please don't beat me," pleaded the boy with folded hands.

Heedless to his pleas for mercy, the stepfather pulled out his army issued belt from his waist with one hand while the other kept on twisting Karma's ears again and again. "I swear I didn't do anything wrong today, *apa*. I swear I didn't do anything wrong," repeated the boy.

"You, worthless creature! You are trying to take sides with your mother, ha! You want to turn against me, ha!"

accused the ex-military man flinging the puny terrified boy half way across the floor.

"No, *apa!* No. I beg of you! Please don't beat me," pleaded Karma again as the man curled the end of the belt devoid of the metal buckle around his shaking palm.

"Leave Karma alone, you drunkard! Leave my son alone!" protested the desperate mother banging on the door, and continued to call for help.

The stepfather beat up the boy till he was too tired to hit the helpless boy anymore. Finally, help arrived in the form of Singye and his wife Kunzang. They knocked on the door again and again, and pleaded the drunkard within to spare the boy. The drunkard finally lifted the half-unconscious boy by his belt, opened the door and dumped him in front of his wife. As Karma murmured his mother's name, as if in his sleep, Kunzang lifted the boy and buried him in her embrace. "*Lama kheno!*" exclaimed Kunzang and started to weep like a child as her heart over flew with sympathy for the boy.

Singye shook his head from side to side with disgust, and remarked, "How could you do such horrible things to your wife and innocent child, Dawa!"

"Singye, just mind your own business, alright! Or else!" warned his neighbour at the top of his voice, steaming with fury, and pointing his index finger at him.

"You are worst than a wild dog, Dawa!" retaliated Singye with a sudden burst of anger uncharacteristic of him. "You are lucky that sister Choiki is not my blood sister," he warned Dawa with the realisation that he had no right to interfere in the matter since he was but just a friendly neighbour.

"What could you have done for her if she were your blood sister, ha!" challenged Dawa.

"Please, brother Singye!" pleaded Choiki as Singye helped her onto her feet.

"Stop this nonsense, the two of you!" demanded Kunzang through her sobs.

"If you think you are man enough, come and talk to me when you are sober, you heartless drunkard," roared Singye accepting the challenge.

"Go away, all of you! Get out of my premises!" yelled Dawa as he turned away and slammed the door behind him.

"Shame on you, Dawa. Shame on you," cursed Singye as he led his helpless neighbours away to the refuge of his own house.

By the time they were near Singye's house, Karma had fully regained consciousness. "Please, put me down, aunt Kunzang. Put me down. I am fine now," he struggled.

"Now, just calm down and relax, my little hero!" cooed Kunzang with unhidden love and sympathy for the boy.

Once inside her house, Kunzang set him up near the oven, and hurriedly prepared a bed. Then, she urged Choiki to lie down in the bed. She also cleaned Choiki's face and wound with warm water and applied some ground-dried bear's gall to the wound. "This will help the wound to heal faster," she consoled her friend.

"I saw a leather belt lying on the floor in the kitchen," remarked Singye. "Don't tell me that he hit you again with the buckle of the belt?" he inquired of Karma.

As Karma nodded his head, Singye started to undo Karma's belt.

"The mushrooms!" murmured Karma pointing his small index finger coated with his mother's blood at his pouch.

"You mean you still have them in your pouch?" asked Singye with a startle.

"Yes, uncle Singye. I held onto it tightly when I was tossed around," exclaimed Karma with his hands crossed over and tightly holding the front pouch of his garment to gesture what he had done. "You said aunt Kunzang will..." he tailed off feeling a little ashamed.

"How I wish Kunzang and I had a son like Karma, sister!" Singye commended Karma's love for his mother, as he emptied Karma's pouch into a bamboo basket. Choiki started to sob without uttering a word. "And, yes! Aunt Kunzang will definitely cook them for your *ama*," he reassured the boy.

Singye stripped Karma naked and inspected the boy's body carefully for the presence of any open wounds. When he was satisfied that there were none, he said, "You are a strong and lucky boy, Karma!"

"Lucky?" protested his wife. "May be strong, but definitely not lucky. Would he have gotten a stepfather as cruel as a wild dog if he was lucky!"

"Come now, Kunzang!" fumbled her husband.

"Poor boy, how much it must have hurt!"

"He is a little black and blue, but as I have already said he is a strong boy. He'll be fine, won't you, Karma?" demanded Singye.

"Yes, uncle Singye. I can even bring more mushrooms tomorrow," replied the boy.

Kunzang did not only cook the mushrooms for dinner that evening but also heated up some locally distilled wine with eggs fried in fresh cow's butter. She forced Choiki to drink three wooden bowls of the wine saying, "Drink it while it is still hot. It'll soothe your body, and you can have a good night's sleep."

Later that night when Karma had laid down beside his mother to sleep, his mother held him close to her body and wept. "I am so sorry that you get beaten up by your stepfather all the time for no reasons at all. It's all my fault that I married him."

"But, he doesn't beat me as much as he beats you, *ama!*" Karma consoled his mother. "You know, *ama*, one day when I grow up and become stronger than him, I will beat him up too," he confided in his mother.

"No, Karma, you must not say such a thing. Promise me that you'll never say such a thing ever again," demanded his mother.

"But he beats us every time!" he protested.

"If you retaliate against him, than you will also become a bad man like him. Do you want to be a *horrible man* like him when you grow up?" demanded his mother stressing the words 'horrible man' with a clear intention to sober him down.

"No, *ama*, never. I will never beat my wife and my son when I grow up," promised Karma pensively knowing exactly what his mother wanted to hear him say.

As sleep came, Karma saw himself as a fully-grown up man, tall, handsome and masculine standing beside his mother in their kitchen. His mother was sitting on an elaborately designed Tibetan carpet by the window merrily singing a song. His stepfather was desperately trying to make a fire at the oven, blowing into the smoke pathetically, his eyes filled with tears, just like his mother's used to be when he was a child. To this, he let out a mild laughter of jubilation in his sleep. And as his dream continued, he saw a huge bamboo basket full to the brim with his mother's favourite species of wild mushrooms in the middle of the kitchen.

The sun was almost up as Choiki lay against a pillow tugged up against the wall beside her bed. Karma was sleeping as calmly as a glacial lake in the northern mountains. The blanket over him heaved in slow motion as he took long rhythmic breaths. Normally he would be up at this time, piously refilling the seven brass cups in their alter room with fresh water from the stream and burning hand-made incense in a small earthen pot of red-hot coals. Then as Choiki closed her eyes against the recurring flashbacks of the previous night's incidents, her mind floated back years into her life to the times when she was a happily married teenager.

She was only seventeen when Rabgay, a young handsome and talented teenager from a well to do family from the village on the other side of the mountain, succeeded impressing her during an encounter at a local festival against the jealousy of half a dozen suitors. And why wouldn't she be impressed with him anyway! After all, he was the most handsome looking teenage boy in all the seven nearby villages put together including her own village. Rabgay also had the etiquette of a noble man that impressed even the Governor of their district. Within a matter of just a few weeks after their encounter, Rabgay had managed to express his feelings for her to his parents. His parents in turn were just as happy to have Choiki, the only daughter of a rich retired King's Chamberlain as their daughter-in law.

Karma was born to them within a year of their marriage to the joy of every kith and kin. He was cared for and loved by his parents, grandparents, uncles and aunts, cousins and his father's servants like a first-born prince to whom the throne was his birthright. There were three years of unshaken pomp and harmony in her husband's house, and undaunted romance between her and Rabgay. But her happy days were as short-lived as a beautiful multihued rainbow around the sun on a sunny drizzling day. While on a trip to a nearby village, Rabgay met an untimely death when his riding pony threw him off a rocky cliff into the reckless river below. The pony had panicked at the sight of a snake in the middle of the narrow mule track on the cliff. Rabgay's body was swallowed by the river, and never found. And she and Karma were thrown out of her husband's house by her in-laws calling her a witch and her son a devil. They had held her and her son's ill luck responsible for Rabgay's death. By then, both her parents had demised, and her father's younger brother had already usurped all her inheritance. Her husband had just started a negotiation with her uncle about her inheritance before he had died.

Choiki was only twenty years old as she walked away with humiliation and despair from her husband's village with a two-year-old son on her back. She had neither a copper coin to her name nor a roof over her head. Had it not been for her son, she would have jumped off the same cliff that had taken her husband's life and followed her husband to heaven. That day, when she had reached her village, all her relatives had turned their backs on her. Her uncle had denied her entrance to her own house even at her pleading. Then, Singye and his wife had come to her rescue. Singye had even laid claim to her inheritance, on her and Karma's behalf, and when her uncle would not budge, he had approached the village elders. Ultimately, her uncle had returned to her an almost empty house, some land and half a dozen cattle from a herd of more than four scores.

Singye and his wife had known about almost everything her parents had possessed- her mother's jewellery, four leather bags of silver coins, three antique gold statues, seven bronze statues, a dozen antique hand-painted and embroidered paintings, about two scores of ivory and maple cups and bowls, her father's three ceremonial swords with silver sheath carved in exquisite designs of gold, all the paraphernalia of their alter which was the largest and had the riches contents in the village, and a hundred and one other things- that her uncle had virtually robbed her of. They had suggested that she appeal to the Governor for justice, pledging their full support for her. But she had turned a deaf ear to their suggestion in fear of destroying the moral respect between her and her uncle. She had also never ever given a thought to claiming Karma's inheritance from her husband's family for the same reason. Over the years she had often felt that her sacrifices were not being rewarded, but she blamed it all on her past *karma* and put her faith in the hands of the Three Jewels.

As the bright rays of the morning sun peered through the open window and fell on Karma's eyes, he sat up in his bed with a startle. He looked around the room with a surprise look on his face as he tried to make out where he was. Within a few heartbeats, he realised his where about and for a moment there he wished that he had died in his sleep. Just then, he felt his mother's warm hand on his head, and he was already looking forward to another day.

"Do you feel alright?" asked his mother in a sad tone.

"Yes, *ama*," lied the faithful son. His body was aching all over, especially his back that gave him an uncomfortable feeling of sharp recurring flashes of momentary aches and a sort of numbness at the same time. "*Lama, ama!* The cattle!" panicked Karma staring at the rays of the sun beaming into the room through the open window. It was almost time to untether the cattle and drive them to the forest to forage.

"Don't worry. Brother Singye has offered to look after our cattle today. In fact, he might have already finished milking them by now. So you have the whole day to yourself."

"No, *ama*," protested the boy. "I am alright. I will take the cows to the forest," declared the boy.

"But...?"

"No, *ama*! I will go," insisted Karma.

As Choiki looked on from the window, Karma had a hasty conversation with Singye. Then, Karma hurriedly limped after their herd of twelve cattle. Karma waved a long shaft of dry dogweed stem and slowly headed towards the forest, and disappeared from her view.

"Karma just wouldn't let me go after the herd!" complained the elderly man to her as he entered the house, shaking his head from side to side like a bullock who has just been stuck hard on the horn with the blunt edge of a butcher's knife. "And why are you on your feet? You are supposed to be in bed," he demanded with the tone of a loving father.

"I am fine, brother. I am really fine now." It was her turn to convince him.

"Don't tell me you are going back to your house now!" demanded her fatherly neighbour with a deep look of concern on his face.

"He must be hungry by now. I am sure that he has not eaten a morsel last night," replied Choiki avoiding his eyes. Her husband had smashed the aluminium pot in which she had cooked the rice and the earthen pot of dry fish and potato curry, with a block of firewood, spilling everything onto the ash outside the oven, before hitting her with it as she tried to save a pot of fermented cheese.

"You will never change, Choiki! And he is not just about to change either!" remarked Singye gutturally as if talking to himself.

"Poor woman!" murmured Singye involuntarily to himself with remorse. "If only her parents were alive!"

And, he imagined how her father would have thrown Dawa out of his house if Dawa had but dared touch even a hair on his dear daughter's body. After all, he had brought her up like a princess, and he had done everything he could to see to it that his Choiki never shed a tear. Then as he recollected her father's childish act one fateful morning, he let out a mild solitary laughter. Choiki's father had incinerated a beautiful mattress made of sheep's wool, out of anger when he saw red marks from flea's bites on his three year-old daughter's body for the fourth morning in a row.

"If only her father were alive!" he wished again as his eyes fell on Choiki slowly sipping a wooden cup of steaming maize powder porridge that his wife had served her.

Then, Singye's forehead was a sight of unruly terraces of a paddy field as he forged his weather beaten brown skin on his forehead into half a dozen wrinkles at the thought of Dawa. Dawa came from a middle class family from a nearby village west of his own. Not long ago, he was a promising young soldier until the day he had to desert the army in fear of the worst when he lost one of the rare rifles while on a patrolling duty along the borders in the north. He had been a renegade for six years. Then, after the army gave up their pursuit on him and dropped the case, he decided to come back to his village. He had earned the respect of his village folks by working in his parent's fields from dawn till dusk for two years. It was then that he had fallen in love with Choiki. After several attempts to win Choiki's heart had failed, Dawa had approached Singye for help with eager promises to take good care of her and be a good father to Karma. Choiki had consented to the proposal when he had reasoned out that it was not wise for a young beautiful widow with a four-year old son to remain single and run her household all by herself. Such a thing attracted the attention of lecherous and unfaithful men, and gossips from the village folks. He also reasoned that Karma must have a man by his side to grow up. Besides, the presence of a man by her side would boost her and Karma's social status. She would also need someone to help her trill the fields and look after the cattle. And, Dawa was just about the right man.

It was not until a year after Choiki's marriage to Dawa that Singye and all the village folks knew about Dawa's drinking habits coupled up with eight years of contained frustrations at his own life. Dawa had never gotten over the traumas he had gone through during his years as a renegade. And he had made his own wife and stepson the victims of his frustrations. When Singye had seen enough of Dawa's animate behaviour and misconduct, he had approached Dawa and tried to sober him down, but in vain. When he proposed Choiki to get a divorce, Choiki would not listen to him. "Dawa has had a bad past. I know that deep inside he is a good man. He will behave himself once he stops drinking," was Choiki's decision.

However, although Dawa would promise to stop drinking and apologise to her for his misconduct every morning when he was sober, he would religiously start the day by "Just one cup to get over last night's hang-over."

... the forest also gave him a lot of wild mushrooms to take home.

And, the story had never changed.

"If only I had not trusted Dawa that fateful day!" regretted Singye as Choiki painstakingly got up on her feet and started for the door.

It was already well past midday, and the shadows of the trees around him were rapidly growing in height and racing towards the east. Karma sat on a rock, his chin resting on his crouched knees held together in the embrace of his hands. He was lost in a thought of his own. His untouched *bangchu* of packed lunch, which Kunzang had tugged into his pouch that morning against his refusal lay carelessly beside him getting colder by the minute. Metomo, the flowery one, the cow in white coat with black spots, passed by the rock slashing through the thick undergrowth of bamboo. After a while, her calf eagerly galloped after her, distracting him for a moment. Karma's eyes lethargically followed the two-some, and his face glowed with a momentary smile. "Just like me and my mother!" Karma spoke aloud. But then again, as the rueful scenes from the previous night replayed in his mind, he spoke aloud again with a deep sigh of repentance, "Only that they don't have a stepfather who beats them up all the time."

His eyes scanned the forest around him, unconsciously trying to distract himself from his own agony. A few heads of his cattle were still within the reach of his view. Two of them were lying down and ruminating casually, half hidden in a thicket of undergrowth while others were busy selectively grazing the young tender leaves of bamboo. Shawala, the bull calf with long legs and roan coat that made him look like a deer, was practising his race joyfully running from one end of a small open ground to another and back again with his tail raised high in the air. Yes, the forest was the place where Karma could either drown himself in his own sorrows or steal a portion of the forest's peace for himself, alone. Alone, with nobody to beat him up, with no one around to insult him and with no need to look at his mother's sufferings. If he felt the need to talk to someone, he could always talk to the trees, the birds, the rocks, and his cattle. They always listened to him. They never shouted at him the way his stepfather did. And they never insulted him like the village children who made fun of him by teasing him about his stepfather thrashing him up. They did not call him and his mother by abusive names either. The forest was his refuge. The forest was good to him. The forest left him alone and never bothered him. And the forest also gave him a lot of mushrooms to take home.

"Mushrooms!" he gasped as his heart started to beat at an unusually fast rate as he suddenly remembered his promise. "Mushrooms!"

He stood erect on the rock and held his breath as if to take a dip in a pool. After twenty heartbeats or so, he released his breath and started sniffing the cold forest air like a wild dog trying to trace the trial of a frail tick-ridden stray calf. And as he picked up a familiar fragrance, he jumped off the rock and dashed towards the source of the scent.

Yet again, all the cows have been tethered in their usual spot in the shed, and all the calves were in the barn just as the sun was kissing the tip of the western mountains. And Karma headed home whistling to the tune of a familiar song. As he was walking past a thicket of oaks, a surprised jungle fowl panicked at his approach and hastily flew off and landed in a thicket at about a quarter of a village archer's shooting distance. And, suddenly his face cracked into a broad smile as he remembered the lyrics of the local song to whose tune he was whistling. "*Jamo nymla phur song, gongdo sala lue song* (The bird has flown off into the sky. The egg is left on earth)."

He continued walking awkwardly and whistling softly to himself again. And as he neared his house, his hands automatically lifted the front pouch of his garment again for the hundredth time as if to guess the weight of its content. Then, he peeped into the pouch, almost toppling off the narrow path as he tipped off a twig, and giggled to himself with a sense of satisfaction. "Of course, they are there!" he smiled feeling reassured. "Where would they go? They can't run and they can't fly. They are just mushrooms."

And, the mushrooms were for his mother.

***

# *Apa Nadola's obsession*

*Apa* Nadola, the Bear Slayer. *Apa* Nadola, the Bear Wrestler. *Apa* Nadola, the Crow. *Apa* Nadola, the Gorilla. *Apa* Nadola, the Simpleton. He was known by these many names by his village folks and to people far and wide. To those who have not had the pleasure, or the displeasure, of an encounter with him, the colourful titles he held and the mean nicknames he was known by did not seem to match altogether. Nevertheless, the tales about his fights with the bears were as eerie and fascinating as could be, or a subject of utmost curiosity even to a highly rational man.

Years after I had heard of the tales about *Apa* Nadola, and forgotten half of them, I was transferred as an agriculture extension agent to Tangmachu. Tangmachu was a village with beautiful rice terraces, equally beautiful ladies who sang like cuckoos and danced like the Indian peacocks, and 60 proof wines expertly brewed from rice and millet. A couple of weeks after I had settled down in a small cottage, I was in Phagidung, a nearby sister-village of Tangmachu, to conduct a day's farmers' training on kitchen gardening. As I was scribbling down the names of the farmers participating in the training in a government-issued spiral notebook with a Nu. 4 ballpoint pen, a man in a well worn-out black cotton *gho* with a white cotton cloth patch the size and shape of a medium-sized *bangchu* on the front pouch of his garment, approached me. I was a little taken aback by his shorter than the normal stature and unusually tar-black complexion like a

Bumtab's sun scorched-resin-smeared face in winter. There he stood in front of me with his feet close together like a soldier at 'Attention' and his upper body bowed forward like an eighty-year old woman. The sleeve of his right hand was covering his mouth while the left arm was neatly stretched and plastered against his left thigh.

"Nadola *la, lopon*," he reported, bowing even lower.

"*Apa* Nadola, the Bear Wrestler, Sir," seconded the village headman, followed by controlled laughter from the elderly men and girlish giggles from the young ladies in the crowd that made *Apa* Nadola move a step forward and a step backward.

"Nervous," I thought observing the man closely from the corner of my eyes, but pretending that I have not noticed anything of interest to me. "Nervous and shy," I concluded secretly in my mind.

"*Apa* Nadola!" I repeated as I jotted down his name. "*Apa* Nadola, please take a sit."

And I was lost in a though of my own. "Phagidung is *Apa* Nadola's locality," I thought aloud with an almost blank mind.

However, the tightening of the muscles in my abdomen suggested that my curiosity was trying to get better of me. Or was it just my failure to fathom the crowd's trying to ridicule *Apa* Nadola, or my forced decency as not to provoke the village headman in particular and or *Apa* Nadola himself to tell me his tales and give the crowd the pleasure of ridiculing him any further? Nevertheless, I could see why *Apa* Nadola was nick named 'the Crow,' and 'the Gorilla,' and 'the Simpleton' as well. His looks and his carriage said it all.

During the lunch break, *Apa* Nadola was sitting right in front of me with a small cotton cloth, as worn out and soot ridden as an overused kitchen towel, of steaming red rice on his lap and a huge wooden cup that was half devoid of the lacquer polish full of curry cupped in his left hand. He was piously crunching on a piece of bone with a yogi's concentration. It seemed as though he was least interested in others' conversations and gossips. And, for a moment, my eyes were magically fixed on *Apa* Nadola.

"Have you heard of his tales, *lopon*?" asked the village headman who was sitting beside me, noticing me staring at *Apa* Nadola.

"Yes. Long time ago," I replied, feeling a bit embarrassed that he had caught me staring at *Apa* Nadola. "Are they true?" I inquired without a second thought, feeling embarrassed even more after my uncontrollable curiosity has gotten better of me.

"Yes, *lopon*," he said with a tune of reassurance as if to say 'I can bet on that!' "Except for the bear slaying part," he added quickly.

"What do you mean?" I whispered leaning over to his side, with a huge piece of red chilly in between my thumb and the index finger half way to my mouth.

"He is not a Bear Slayer," he declared. "Least kill a bear, he can't even kill a flea that sucks his blood and takes away his sleep at night," he continued. "He is a very religious man, I must say, *lopon*."

"*Aayee!*" I agreed half-heartedly. Of course, I was not sure whether Sonam was trying to protect *Apa* Nadola or really conveying me the truth since my experiences with farmers told me that they would seldom share a story about killing a wild animal with a civil servant, least with an official of the Ministry of Agriculture. They were well aware that killing a bear required a lot of justifications by the law.

"But he sure does wrestle with bears," he said. "He has already wrestled and defeated nine bears during the last twenty seven years," exclaimed Sonam with a tone of appreciation.

"Really!" I gasped, almost spitting out the chilly I had just chewed up.

"He is obsessed with this wrestling. He wouldn't even wrestle with a village kid though. He is shy, humble and timid, you see," he went on.

"Interesting man!" I remarked.

"But he is getting old now. He is already 52," he said with a sad tone full of concern for the man.

"Do you think he will wrestle with a bear again?" I asked without any attempt to hide my excitement.

"Yes, *lopon*. He sure will. Come August, September, and he will be on the lookout in the maize fields, and the village youngsters will be after him for the fun of it all again. The youngsters will even try to find a bear so that they can witness the wrestling, you see," he confided. "They just can't understand that by doing this they are putting Nadola's life in danger," he complained with a tone of distaste. "Now that the numbers of wild dogs have decreased drastically during the last one decade, our fields are a second home to the deer, wild boars and the bears. Nadola will encounter more and more of them now, and easily too," he reasoned giving me a pinch of his pool of knowledge befitting a man with 50 years of stay on mother earth to boast with in front of a 28 year-old young freak like myself.

"But he is getting old," he said again almost in a murmur after a long silence. It was as clear as the Evening Star on a cloudless night that this man admired *Apa* Nadola, and was full of concern for him.

"*Lopon*, pardon me if I am mistaken, but I think you would love to see the match yourself," he said taking me by surprise, at the end of the day's training. And before I could utter a word he added, "I will inform you of his next 'wrestling match' if I know when it is going to take place in advance. Sometimes, we do."

One early September noon while I was in my office, a boy knocked at the door and greeted me. "*Kuzuzangpo la, lopon!* I am Phagidung Village Headman's son. My father has sent me to request *lopon* to come to our house this evening," he said.

I almost asked of the boy "Why does he want me?" when I remembered what the Village Headman had promised me the last time we had met.

While Sonam and I were on third round of *ara*, *Apa* Nadola walked into the room, greeted me courteously with a big smile, and sat beside Sonam with the same wooden cup, the one he was using during the training the first and the last time I saw him, in his hand. Sonam filled up his cup, turned to me, and announced, "He is my elder brother."

And I wondered why he had waited so long to tell me that.

"He is going to wrestle with a big one tonight. He just won't listen!" he said with a heavy sigh after taking a few sips of *ara*.

"*Apa* Nadola, why do you do this? It's too dangerous," I remarked without giving him a chance to answer my question. "At your age, it's just too risky, if you don't mind my saying," I tried to caution him.

"Yes, *lopon*. What you say is right, *lopon*," he replied in a low voice. "Tonight will be the last one. After this I will not fight a bear again," he declared. And my instinct told me that no one could make him change his mind. Not tonight. *Apa* Nadola had already made up his mind.

"She is going to come back tonight. She was there last night, in that maize field. No one disturbed her, and she had her fill. Yes, *lopon*, she'll be back tonight. Bears always come back for more," *Apa* Nadola stated, full of excitement, sharing with me a piece of his experience with a bear's behaviour.

"But, *achey*, she is a full grown young bear. She might even be a mother. She could be very dangerous!" the younger brother protested.

"I know that. You just keep away while I wrestle with her. And keep *lopon* at a safe distance," he cautioned.

When we reached the maize field on the outskirts of the village, Sonam and I climbed a huge peach tree at the edge of the field while *Apa* Nadola hid himself in a bush of dogweed. Before we went our ways, Sonam shoved his dragger into his elder brother's hand. "At least take this. I know you didn't bring yours," suggested Sonam almost pleading.

The elder brother waved it away without a word. And the long wait began.

The night was deafly quiet except for an occasional hustling of the leaves on the tress to the pleasant humming of the cold night wind. The moon shone brightly in an ocean of white, blue and red stars. Trees cast ghostly shadows around them. I peered towards *Apa* Nadola's hideout, and to my surprise he was standing in the middle of the bush.

"Do you reckon that *Apa* Nadola has sensed the bear's arrival?" I whispered to Sonam.

They started rolling down the sloppy maize field.

He followed the direction of my vision and asked, "Why, *lopon*?"

"Why is he standing there?" I asked.

"Where, *lopon*?" Sonam answered me with another question after his eyes had combed the place that I had directed to him with my index finger.

"There! There!" I pointed toward *Apa* Nadola again.

Just then, I realised that the figure was too tall to be *Apa* Nadola. Just too tall! "I think that is not *Apa* Nadola," I remarked. "Were you expecting any company?"

"No, *lopon*. Nobody knows about this," he assured. And, I don't see nobody around either," he added, the sign of height of patience clear in the tone of his voice.

Just then, I saw the silhouette walk away towards the middle of the field. "There he is. See?" I whispered to Sonam frantically pointing towards the silhouette again. "Look, he is walking into the maize field."

Again, Sonam scanned the direction I had given him from every possible angle, and said, "No, I don't see anybody around. You might have seen a moving shadow, *lopon*."

And, as I watched on, the silhouette vanished into the maize field.

After a while that seemed like eternity, an owl hooted in the distance. This was followed by a single gust of wind that kept the maize plants swaying from side to side while their dry leaves made noises like that of half a dozen cattle walking through heaps of dry oak leaves. "Something is not right tonight!" I thought aloud. And the very thought released a gush of adrenaline in my veins that made my mouth dry and every hair on my body rise. When the owl hooted again, the man next to me threw a quizzical look at me and murmured, "*Om ah hung baza guru padma sedy hum. Om ah hung...*"

Just as I was trying to calm myself down, I heard a cracking sound in the filed. When we looked towards it, not more than 100 yards away was the bear. Her eyes were glowing red in the moonlit night as she stood up on her hind legs and pulled down a bunch of maize plants. Then, I saw *Apa* Nadola walking swiftly but casually towards the bear, like a schoolchild walking to a match of basketball game. When *Apa* Nadola was about 40 yards away, the bear seemed to have noticed his presence. She stopped gnawing at the fallen maize plants, and looked towards *Apa* Nadola. As he continued his approach, she raised her muzzle and growled at him with the shake of her head. As *Apa* Nadola sped up his pace, she took a step backward and growled again. The bear's white fangs shone in the moonlight. Then, to my surprise, *Apa* Nadola raced toward the bear. And before the bear could take a decision between 'fight and flight,' *Apa* Nadola was face to face with the bear, his eye fixed on her, his arms extended at an angle to his body and his upper frame slightly bowed forward as if to jump at her. The bear rose on her hind legs and growled at the top of her voice again. That almost shook me off the peach tree. Then, to my utmost astonishment, *Apa* Nadola let out a shrill cry, like some war cry from a soldier in battle, lunged at the bear and held her tight with his arms around the bear's waist in a tight embrace. The man and the beast had just declared war on each other.

My mouth went dry again, and my grip on the branch tightened at the sight of her full body length. She was at least half a dozen inches taller than *Apa* Nadola. In a flash *Apa* Nadola plastered himself against the shiny white undercoat of the bear, his arms holding his opponent tight, his grip firm and strong as an iron chain.

"The match begins now," announced my companion.

"What do we do?" I managed to ask through my quivering lips.

"Nothing, *lopon*. Just stay put and watch," replied Sonam.

By then the man and the beast were struggling hard trying to overpower one another. The bear was desperately trying to gnaw her opponent's head with her powerful fangs. *Apa* Nadola who was well aware of the bear's intentions had his head tugged up tightly and safely against her throat, his powerful hand holding the bear's neck in a tight embrace. Every time the bear tried to send him down on his knees by leaning forward and putting the full weight of her body on her opponent, *Apa* Nadola pulled her down hard on to his head choking her with every pull. The puny man also did not give her any chance to rip his body apart with her claws as he kept sending her off balance time and again by swinging her around. All she could do for the moment was retaliate his physical prowess with her own and wait for the precise moment for him to make a mistake and expose his head or body for her to gnaw on or claw at. After a while, *Apa* Nadola was panting very fast and sweating profusely as he kept swinging the bear around. He seemed to know that he must tire out the bear before she could get him.

The night was filled with the noise of the bear's growl, *Apa* Nadola's war-cry like sound, the cracking noise of the breaking maize plants, the thuds of the bear's weight against the ground every time *Apa* Nadola lifted and swung her and tried to nail her to the ground, and the crushing and cracking sound of dry maize leaves and plants as the two either trampled or shook them. After wrestling for almost 10 minutes, the two fell to the ground, *Apa* Nadola on top of her, still holding tight on to her body. Then, they started rolling down the sloppy maize field, felling all the maize plants along the way. Finally, they fell down the cliff at the edge of the field and disappeared from our view.

"*Lopon*, I think we better go after them," suggested Sonam. "But please stay close to me, and be alert," he cautioned.

Shaking all over, I climbed down the tree, and ran after Sonam to the edge of the field from where the two had fallen off. As we looked down the cliff, our vision of the bottom of the cliff where we expected to find the two was blocked by a group of bamboo. Just then, we heard a loud crashing noise, and a loud and shrill growl of a beast followed by the cry of a man in great agony.

"I think they have landed near the bamboo stumps down there," Sonam said in a low murmur. "We cannot make it there directly from here. The cliff is very steep and pretty high. We will have to take the longer route around the cliff."

By the time we reached the bottom of the cliff, a small group of men from the village had already gathered at the scene. As I followed their eyes, my eyes rested near a man with a huge torch of pine flint in his right hand held head high. In front of him were the motionless bodies of the bear and *Apa* Nadola perched upon a group of bamboo stumps. *Apa* Nadola's arms were still around the bear. As I walked closer and saw blood running down the bamboo stumps beneath the warriors' bodies, my heart was in my throat. And at a distance, the owl hooted again, and as I looked up the cliff, I saw the silhouette walking casually up the rocky cliff as if the cliff were a red carpet floor in a king's palace.

***

# *The devilish inheritance*

"Sonaaaaammm! *Wai*, Soonaaammm! Come and have your lunch now!" called a familiar voice from a distance. And, the message seemed to echo from the walls and roofs of every house in the village.

"That's my mother. I have got to go now," announced Sonam Deki excitedly with a twinkle in her eyes. She carefully laid down the miniature baby doll that she had forged out of a puddle of mud in front of Zangmo, her closest friend in the whole wide world. Still sitting on a plank of wood, she reached out to a large young duck-weed beside her and plucked it clean off the plant. As she got up on her feet and wiped the mud off her small hands with the leaf exposing her egg white skin while simultaneously getting up on her feet to leave, she flung a casual look at her friend. "I am starving," she confided in her friend.

"Alright! Go ahead. I will wait here for you," Zangmo assured her friend with a smile that could have melted even the devil's heart.

She picked up the mud baked baby doll and wrapped it neatly with a piece of pink polyester cloth that she had picked up on her way to the play-site from the rubbish pit outside tailor Sangay's house. "Since your mother is going to call you any time now, why don't you go home too, and we'll meet here again after lunch," suggested Sonam.

"No, I don't feel like eating. I feel as if my tummy is full," countered Zangmo with a heavy sigh. "I saw that dream again last night, you see," confided Zangmo in a sad tone.

"Oh, I am so sorry for you, Zangmo!" exclaimed Sonam with a look of genuine concern on her face. "Why don't you come with me to my place to eat. May be a change of place will bring back your appetite."

"That's alright. I really don't feel like eating. You go ahead," declined Zangmo, her eyes unmoving and fixed on the doll.

Sonam sat down beside her mother on the finely polished floor made of rock-hard walnut planks in their kitchen to partake a small circular bamboo basket of cooked ground maize, a maple cup of steaming curry of potato and red chillies dressed with cheese and cup of fresh butter milk. As she started to eat, her mind was preoccupied by her concern for Zangmo. Like herself, Zangmo had also just turned six, and since Zangmo always shared every dream she saw with her, she knew that Zangmo had been seeing more dreams than she did lately. As for her, she would either hardly see any dreams or she could never remember them well enough to share with her friend; she wished she did. However, Zangmo's dreams were most often than not either terrifying or sad. She would either see someone trying to hurt or actually hurting somebody else, or herself trying to run away from someone or something. Such dreams always made Zangmo feel as if she had just been ran over by a herd of mules, the following day. The only supposedly happy dreams she saw were those of herself sharing a lot of food and drinks (although she was too small to even touch liqueur of any kind) with her mother offered by other people. And every time she saw a dream of that nature, she would lose her appetite the next day even if she had gone to bed empty stomach the previous night. So, Sonam always thought that Zangmo saw weird dreams that had weird impacts on her, and always felt sorry for her friend.

One day, while Sonam was amidst laughter and fun at a spinning wheel with her mother spinning wool for her mother to weave a *gho* for her father, Sonam felt a sudden tummy ache. She tried in vain to hide the pain from her mother, but the profuse sweat on her forehead gave away the game.

"*Ya lama*, you are sweating a lot!" exclaimed her surprised mother. "Are you alright?" she continued concurrently placing the back of her palm on her forehead to feel her temperature. "*Ya lama*, you have got a fever," panicked her mother.

"No, *ama*. I just got an abrupt mild tummy ache," she said arduously to calm down her mother.

"Abrupt? Mild? What do you mean? And what about the sweat?" she demanded. "We don't have the fire going, and this isn't summer either!" she continued, and before Sonam could even think of an alibi, her mother threw another question with an inquisitive look on her face, "Have you started getting a visitor already?"

"Who, *ama*?" inquired Sonam nervously.

"I mean, have you already started getting your periods?" rephrased her mother.

"What period, *ama*?" Sonam managed to mutter through her clenched teeth as her face started to redden with the escalating body temperature.

Within a few seconds, the pain became unendurable. Sonam jammed the palms of her hands hard against her tummy in an effort to subdue the discomfort, crouched her body, and rolled over on her side on the bare floor. Her mother quickly lifted Sonam's head, placed it onto her lap, and called out frantically. "Sonam *apa*! Sonam *apa*!" And as her father came dashing into the room, Sonam's mother pleaded to him, "Sonam is sick. Please run to the astrologer and seek his advice."

Dechen laid her daughter on a mattress in the altar room and spread a thick woollen blanket over her. Sonam started shivering uncontrollably as her body temperature suddenly started to drop at a squirrel's pace as if she was immersed naked in a heap of ice on a chilling January morning. Just as the sound of a conch, blown dutifully by a monk outside the village monastery wavered over the valley announcing dusk, Sonam sat up erect in her bed and curiously searched the room with her weak eyes like a monkey introduced to a novel object. Then, she threw her long hair over her shoulder with a swift toss of her head, looked at her mother and gave her a warm familiar smile that surely did not belong to her. Nervously, Dechen held her daughter by her shoulders with both her hands and tried to help her down. "Lay down, and try to get some sleep now. You will feel better when you get up in the morning," she persuaded and tried to keep her daughter's spirits high.

"Is something wrong with me, Dechen?" demanded Sonam in a familiar hoarse voice to her total astonishment. "I don't feel comfortable here," she continued, throwing a brief glance from the corner of her eyes at the one feet tall bronze idol of Tara that was shining in the flickering light of a butter lamp in the altar. "Let's go to your kitchen," she tried to get up, and Dechen's whole self was filled with a cacophony of anguish, despair and anger as she realised what was going on.

Sonam was possessed by Zangmo's mother's evil spirit.

As Sonam's father ran into the room, his wife was screaming at Sonam, so he thought, at the top of her, "You shameless women, how could you do this!"

"Take it easy, Dechen," he put his hand on her shoulder and gently squeezed it hoping to calm her down.

"Sonam is your daughter's best friend, you Fein," yelled Dechen into Sonam's face, tears rolling down her cheeks.

To this, Sonam gave her a sly look and started to sway her head from side to side like a guilty teenage monk thief receiving a lecture from his Lama on good conduct.

"So, you already know!" remarked her husband. "Why don't you calm down and serve our guest some *ara* and food," he suggested, stressing the words '*ara*' and 'food' while his eyes were fixed on the patient full of disgust.

"Dorji, your new-born calf is really beautiful," Sonam said, taking Dorji by surprise.

"So that's the story," exclaimed Dorji as he put a small wooden table in front of her.

Zangmo's mother liked Dorji's newborn mithun crossbred female calf. She must have thought of it or must have been thinking about it at that very moment thereby unconsciously releasing the evil spirit in her to visit his household and harm his daughter.

Dechen put some cold leftover rice from their lunch that afternoon, and a piece of salted dry fish in a clean *bangchu* on a small traditional table in front of her guest. She separated the rice in the *bangchu* through the middle into two equal piles. Then, as she placed a maple cup beside the *bangchu* and filled it up with wine from a cylindrical bamboo container, she started to chant the traditional spell that she was well versed with. She had picked up the spell from her own mother years ago when her mother conducted the rituals to cast away evil spirits that made her sick every now and then when she was a kid.

"Whether you have come from the east or west or north or south, please have *ara* and rice with fish. Whether you have come from Minjay, Tangmachu, Nyiebee, Shungkhar, or Dromashong or from within Phagidung, please drink some wine and eat hot rice and delicious fish. Whether the guest is from far or from near, please quench your thirst with *ara* and dismiss your hunger with rice and fish. Whether you are a spirit of the living or of the dead or of a demi-god, please quench your thirst with wine and dismiss your hunger with rice and fish. But please do not harm us. Do not harm our innocent child. For we have neither the heart of a revengeful son out to avenge his parents' murder nor the grudge of two envious lovers between us. So, please do not harm us. Do not harm our innocent daughter. If our service is not up to your expectations, please do not be upset, forgive us, and do not harm us. Please, look upon yourself, and do not harm others."

Then, she picked up the table with one hand while the other nabbed the edge of Sonam's *kira* as if removing a flea from it. "Now, please leave. Do not harm us. Please go back to where you have come from. Do not harm our innocent daughter, and leave us alone," she requested and ushered an invisible guest out of the room.

As her mother was crossing the threshold of the altar room, Sonam suddenly felt a great sense of relief, as if she has just been released from inside a pot of boiling cauldron. She felt her body drained of every bit of energy, and she slowly slumped on to the mattress. As her father gently stroked her hair with his fingers, and seemed to murmur something, her eyes began to feel heavy. And as she closed her eyes, she saw Zangmo and her mother leaving the altar room. She tried to call after Zangmo, but the weariness of her body and the sleep in her eyes got better of her. Then, she heard her father's murmur fade away into the silence of the night.

Early next morning, Zangmo walked into Sonam's room. "Sonam, I saw you in my dream last night. You were very sick. Are you alright?" she asked.

For a moment, Sonam was almost staring into her friend's face, and she was lost in a thought of her own as she vaguely recalled last night's incident. She had seen Zangmo and her mother leaving the altar room at the end of the ritual, and she knew that they could not have been in their house in person last night because she was alone with her parents. Then, as her experiences from the previous night began to reveal an unbearable truth, she felt utterly sorry for herself and even sorrier for her friend. What she had been hearing from her parents and other village folks about Zangmo's family was true after all. Then, she realised that Zangmo was going to inherit the family's evil spirit of the living. In fact, she might already have. And, as she recollected Zangmo's tales of her dreams, the thought of the possibilities of her friend already possessing the evil spirit became even more. "*Lama kheno*, not her! Not my best friend!" she pleaded deep inside her heart.

A flood of saline tears washed down her cheeks. She felt her stomach churning with a mind of its own. Her heart ached unbearably as if her bare chest was cut open and her very heart slashed through by a sharp dragger. "She is so nice, so gentle, so loving and so beautiful.

And she is the closest friend I have. Why her, *Kencho sum*? Why my Zangmo?" she continued pleading at the back of her mind, her mouth wide open with despair.

And, the room was suddenly filled with her uncontrollably desperate sobs as she released the tension in her, and reached out to Zangmo with her extended arms as though Zangmo were her prince charming who has come to her rescue. Zangmo knelt down and took her into her gentle arms. And, through her sobs, Sonam reassured Zangmo, "I am alright! I am alright, Zangmo."

Sonam cried her despair out in her friend's loving arms. But she kept what she saw the other night to herself, least she would offend her friend. Deep in her heart, she wished desperately that she had not seen what she really had. And pathetically tried to convince herself that what she thought she saw the other night actually did not happen. "No, it didn't. It can't happen. It shouldn't happen. Not to Zangmo. And not between us," she lamented, and cried even more as her friend tried to calm her down, without the faintest idea of what was torturing Sonam deep inside of her. "No matter what, Zangmo will always be my best friend," decided Sonam secretly.

One day, as Sonam was weaving a *kira* beside her mother, "Sonam, you are eighteen now. Soon you will be married and have a family of your own," said her mother without looking at her, takin her by surprise.

"So, *ama*?" teased Sonam.

"I really feel that you should stop befriending Zangmo," she said as a matter of fact.

"Please, *ama!* Not again! She is the closest friend I have got," complained Sonam hysterically.

"I know, but village folks say that her evil spirit is getting more powerful than even that of her mother's. It could be dangerous for you. It could be dangerous for our family. They say that her evil spirit can now even walk the nights in the form of a fierce looking bear," her mother tried to convince her.

"It is nonsense, *ama!* Stop saying cruel things about my friend," she yelled back, took off the leather strap from her waist, dumped the half-finished *kira* on the floor, and dashed out of the room.

Sonam ran out the village and up a hillock to her favourite hangout-spot under the old wild pear tree on the cliff. That was the place where the gently blowing cold winds from the snow-capped mountains in the far north of her village always made her headaches of frustrations and heartaches of sorrows fly away. As she approached the spot, she saw Zangmo sitting there all alone staring at an eagle hovering in the clear afternoon sky. Sonam excitedly ran up the rest of the cliff.

"What are you doing here alone!" asked Sonam through a halting breath.

"How I wish I were that eagle!" Zangmo said in a soft and tired voice, her eyes fixed on the eagle that was hovering gaily in the blue sky while her hands were cupped on her well-proportioned chin and her elbows rested on her bent knees. "I could just fly away, far away from this village and from everybody," she continued with a tone of deep remorse in her voice.

"And, leave me all alone here staring at another eagle!" teased Sonam. "If your wish comes true, I will also make the same wish. And if my wish should also be granted, I will fly after you," continued Sonam trying to cheer up her friend.

"Why would you want to do that?" asked Zangmo.

"Because you are my best friend, and I want to be near you always," replied Sonam sounding like an eight-year old girl.

"Really!" exclaimed Zangmo with a blank mind.

"Anything the matter?" asked Sonam feeling concerned.

"Would you promise not to tell anyone if I told you something?" demanded Zangmo.

Sonam swore to secrecy instantly.

Then, Zangmo took Sonam's hand into hers, looked into her eyes like a starving stray dog begging for food, and asked, "Do you know that my mother has the evil spirit of the living, and that I have it too?" taking Sonam by utmost surprise.

For a minute or so, Sonam was lost for words. Then, as Zangmo's tears fell on her hand, Sonam yelled, "What is wrong with you today? Why are you saying such horrible things?"

"But it's true, Sonam," declared Zangmo. "I realised it completely only last night."

Zangmo started crying like a starving baby from whom somebody has snatched away the milk bottle. "Do you remember the dreams I used to tell you about?" Zangmo asked in between sobs.

"Yes, what about them?"

"The person who was trying to hurt or was hurting other people in my dream was no other than my mother's evil spirit, and *Lama kheno...*" She broke down again.

"Are you crazy? Is this a joke or what, Zangmo? You are imagining things, right?" exclaimed Sonam desperately trying to console her friend.

"No, it is not my imagination, and I am not crazy either," Zangmo defended herself as if she was fully confident of the facts. "And that thing I was trying to run away from in my dreams was my inner-self's fear of my mother's evil spirit initially," explained Zangmo.

"What do you mean by *initially*," demanded Sonam with an eerie air engulfing her entire being that sent a cold chill down her spines.

"That has been ultimately replaced by my own," Zangmo went on. "What am I going to do, Sonam? What am I going to do? I can't bear this thing inside of me hurting innocent people for nothing. Lot of people have already been hurt."

Zangmo leaned over and buried her face in her friend's lap as if trying to escape the sight of a horrible scene. Sonam was lost for words. She tried to fumble for something to say to console her friend but the words choked in her throat. "Last night at around midnight I saw myself walking through the village alone," continued Zangmo. "Every dog in the village started to bark and growl as they saw me walk by. Some of them were chasing me as I started to run. Then, suddenly I saw my body transform into a huge black bear, noticing which the dogs backed away from me and barked even louder. Then, as I, I mean the bear, was passing by *Apa* Norbu's millet field, the bear transformed back into my body. Oh, Sonam, it was so frightening."

Sonam was lost for words again. Zangmo started to cry pathetically again. "Then, as I was walking along the edge of the field, I saw Karma walking towards me," Zangmo continued after a long time. "As I was trying to greet him, he walked right through me as if I was a layer of thin air. At this, I felt a tremendous sense of rage build up inside me, and I saw myself chasing him and scratching his back time and again. Then, this morning I

And, the two friends stared at the eagles in unison...

heard that Karma was sick because his back was badly scratched by an evil spirit last night. I was that evil spirit, Sonam, I," lamented Zangmo hitting her chest with her fist. And as Sonam held Zangmo's hand tightly to stop her friend from hurting herself, "I swear I had no intention of hurting him or anybody else for any reason whatso-ever," she confessed.

Finally, Sonam managed to say, "That wasn't you, and it's not your fault that Karma is sick, Zangmo. Do you hear me! It's not your fault."

"But I saw myself scratching him. I swear I did." And she broke down again.

"Listen to me, Zangmo. I know you wouldn't do such a terrible thing. It wasn't you but the evil spirit inside you. You must understand this. You must believe this," commanded Sonam with genuine concern for her friend and feeling terribly sorry for her.

Then, Sonam herself broke down at the sight of her friend's despair. And there on the cliff, under the old wild pear tree, the two friends lay in each other's arms crying helplessly at Zangmo's devilish inheritance.

A chilling gust of wind announced the approach of winter. Another eagle joined the solitary eagle in the clear sky. The bright rays of the late afternoon sun sent off multicoloured hues of sparkles from the surface of a silver mirror clear river down in the valley. And the two friends stared at the eagles in unison, exchanged a glance with one another, and smiled. Each knew what the other was thinking of. Two friends. Two eagles. One wish.

***

# *Maymay Wamla's umbrella*

In the remote village of Khema, one never saw an umbrella those days. No, not even the riches family in the village had one. When it rained unbearably hard, the village folks would conveniently pull up the upper portions of their dresses over their heads and run for cover. Well, this was something that women could do much easily than men. Not that they were smarter by any degree but merely because of the fact that the *tegus* they wore could be pulled over their heads more conveniently. Like most of the village kids, I would seldom do it. In fact, I would even run out and play in the rain with my playmates. And, of course, we did not heed our mothers' advice to keep out of the rain because against their caution, we never became sick because of the rain. If we ever got sick after playing in the rain, it was because of the cold. But than that is another story!

Well, as I was saying nobody in the village had an umbrella. In fact, I had never seen one till the day *Maymay* Wamla brought one home from Gudama. Like many others from the village, *Maymay* Wamla went to Gudama once every year to trade with the Indians. So, during one of his trips, he had brought home an umbrella. That year, the very next morning after his return from Gudama, he asked me to accompany him to the village's monastery to make some offerings to our Guardian Deities. Full of enthusiasm, I was running all over the house trying to be useful to my mother in packing up a big *bangchu* of rice with some hard boiled eggs, fried dry fish, some garlic leaves, a small *palang* of *ara*, a kettle of melted castor oil, some fruits, candies and biscuits for the monastery. Time and again I dropped a thing or two or tripped over one thing or another trying to get things done a little faster.

"Jigmi, please stop trying to help me or I will see to it that your grandpa goes to the monastery alone. You are not being useful. Just sit beside grandpa and let me do the packing," said my mother repeatedly.

"Listen to your mother, *lepo*, and come and sit here," seconded *maymay* dutifully at last but luring me by secretly showing me a candy without my mother noticing it.

He always addressed me *lepo* and seldom by my given name. I liked it though, since I understood that an elder calls one *lepo* out of love rather than to imply its literary meaning- the dumb. However, unlike other people, except my mother who just addressed *Maymay* as *apa*, I always addressed him *Maymay*, and never used his second name. I did not like it. I mean his second name. I felt bad even when others used it. My grandpa did not look like a bear. So, I would not have anyone called him 'Wamla', the male bear. But than again, he was not the only one who was called a bear. There was also a man called Domchungla, which also meant the same thing. I also had a girl playmate who was nicknamed Domchungmo. That is that about my grandpa's name and the *Dom*s.

Quietly I sat beside him greedily crunching a candy in my mouth. Usually I would rather hold the candy in between my thumb and the forefinger by one end while miserly licking the other end. However, that morning I knew that I could be a little extravagant since I knew

Well, I couldn't help myself from staring at it.

there were more coming. All I had to do to get another one was bother my mother or run all over the place. By the time I had eaten four candies and was pressing my luck for the fifth, we were all set to leave for the monastery.

'WOOP' went up the umbrella followed by a 'DAG.' I took a step backward, stood frozen and stared on quizzically as grandpa hoisted it over his head.

"Come and walk beside me," he beckoned to me.

I stood beside him, my eyes still fixed on the umbrella above our heads. Grandpa held me close to his big masculine thigh with his right hand firmly anchored on my right shoulder while holding the umbrella with his left. As we started to walk, I tripped over a small rock since I was staring at the umbrella rather than concentrating on the footpath.

"*Lepo*, don't stare at the sky while walking," advised grandpa.

"*Maymay*, what is this?" I asked pointing my small index finger at the umbrella after having stared at it for more than five minutes.

"Ah! So you were staring at the *nyendu!*" he concluded.

"*Nyendu?*"

"Yes, this is what it is called," he said. "It gives one shade against the sun and the rain," he introduced me to the function of the umbrella involuntarily.

So, that was that. But I thought it looked wonderful over one's head. And, I moved even closer to grandpa's big thigh not wanting to be outside its cover.

Well, I could not help myself from staring at it. I had seen a similar one, only more colourful, being hoisted over Guru Rinpoche's head by a monk during the Guru Tshen Gey mask dance at the annual *Tshechu* in Lhuntsi Dzong. But that *nyendu* was nothing like that of grandpa's. Unlike that *nyendu*, grandpa's was all black with iron rod frames and a much shorter cane handle that was hooked at the lower end. Furthermore, grandpa's *nyendu* could be conveniently held with just one hand; one did not need a monk to hold it over one's head. It could also be kept hanging from almost anything in the corner of a room while not in use; I guessed that that was the way one could make use of the hooked handle.

However, I was not the only one who was staring at the umbrella with admiration. As grandpa and I walked casually through the village towards the monastery on the hilltop, the sight of the umbrella drew all my play-mates and almost all the children in the village to us. Some kids just could not gather enough guts to approach us, so they looked on sheepishly and shyly from a dis-tance while the others either followed us or walked be-side us or hopped backwards in front of us with their eyes fixed on the *nyendu*.

"This is called a *nyendu*," I taught all the kids.

To those staring from a distance, I even cried out the message at the top of my voice. And all the while grandpa wore a big smile and walked more and more rhythmically like a new army recruit towards the end of his training perfecting the drill in slow motion. Of course, the magic of the umbrella worked on the village elders as well. Some ran out of their houses while others left their milking cows partially milked or their breakfasts half eaten or threw away their farm implements in the field, and ap-proached us to have a closer look at the umbrella. After a while, we were surrounded by at least two dozen men, women and children, and an air of never ending questions ranging from "What is this" and "Where did you get it from?" and "How much have you paid for it?" to "Will you barter it with..." and "Will you sell it?" Grandpa answered everyone's question the best way he could but always emphasising that his umbrella was just for himself and that he would not part with it for anything. Then, people touched it, felt it, and if I should remember correctly, I think some even sniffed at it.

Well, that was not the end of the commotion. Two days later *Ama* Thuji came to see grandpa with a *palang* of wine.

"I have not been able to come and thank you for the dry fish you have sent for me, *Maymay* Wamla," she said sitting face to face with grandpa. "I have nothing to offer to you but some *ara*," she continued as she put the *palang* in-between them. "I don't know how good it is, but I have distilled it this morning from the stock which had been fermented for more than five months," she added as modestly as she could but indirectly (or was it directly?) conveying the message that her wine ought to be quite good.

"You should not have taken the trouble, Thuji," remarked grandpa courteously.

"*Aaah*, it is not often that I have something to offer you, *maymay*," she countered as she served grandpa a cup full from the *palang*.

"Why don't you join me," offered grandpa.

"I think I should not," she pretended to be hesitant. "But may be I will have to keep you company, *maymay*," she added in a haste. "They say that wine is good only as long as you have someone drinking beside you."

"Very true, Thuji," agreed grandpa. "That is a reason more than good enough for you to join me," he added as *Ama* Thuji took out a maple cup from the front pouch of her garment and filled it up.

"*Maymay*, how was your trip to Gudama?" inquired the lady.

"Not too bad," summed up grandpa.

"I was told that you have brought an interesting item from Gudama!" exclaimed the lady blushing slightly.

"Oh, yes. I have brought a *nyendu*."

"I was wondering if I could have a look at it!" requested *Ama* Thuji politely.

"Sure. I will show it to you right away," agreed grandpa getting up instantly and walking into his bedroom to fetch it. "Here it is," announced grandpa as he came out of his room with the umbrella. He put it on and rotated it by stirring it by the hook with his right hand while balancing it with his left. "It is a very handy thing to have, a very convenient thing to carry with oneself. It can be used to protect one from the sun and the rain. It can also be used as a walking stick and to chase away ferocious dogs while travelling places," he lectured.

*Ama* Thuji got up on her feet excitedly and hurried towards grandpa meeting him half way across the room. She reached for the umbrella, and grandpa handed it over to her. She looked at it from every angle, opened it, closed it, opened it again, and hoisted it over her head. Then she sheepishly looked at grandpa, hesitated for a moment and said, "*Maymay*, will you sell it to me by any chance?"

"No, Thuji, I won't," was grandpa's instant answer. "Dorji has even offered me a year old female calf in exchange for it. But I told him that it isn't for sale," added grandpa.

"I will offer you more than what Dorji has," insisted the lady.

"No, I won't part with it for anything," declared grandpa. "It is a gift from an Indian friend across the boarder in Mela Bazaar," he lied. "As you know, one must never part with the gift given to him with love and respect by a friend," he added.

After that, the two did not converse much. They had another round of wine, more out of courtesy than anything else. Right after the last drop of wine in her cup has been gulped down almost urgently, *Ama* Thuji left with the remaining *palang* of wine.

The next morning grandpa wanted to stitch one of his torn garments outside in the sun. He asked me to give him a hand to which I readily agreed. And the help! Well, he wanted to be Guru Rinpoche and me to be the monk holding the umbrella for him while he did the stitching. But honestly, I was treated better than the monk-grandpa at least asked me to stand under the umbrella, and I was happy that he did.

Just then, the village monastery's *Dorji Lopon*, the second in command during religious festivities and rituals in the monastery came by and greeted grandpa who had not even noticed the man.

"*Yaa*, I did not see you, *lopon*," apologised grandpa and returned the elderly man's greetings.

"I was told you came back from Gudama four days ago!" exclaimed the man.

"Yes, *lopon*," replied grandpa.

"So, you have brought this *nyendu* from Gudama?"

"Yes, *lopon*."

"Such a fine piece of equipment!" went on the *lopon*.

"It certainly is, *lopon*," agreed grandpa.

"Useful, rain or shine!"

"It sure is, *lopon*," agreed grandpa again.

"As you know, being the *Dorji Lopon* of our monastery I have to keep on travelling from one village to another to conduct religious rituals for the needy. And I have to do it rain or shine. It is a hard life!" said the *lopon* with a heavy sigh, his eyes unmoving from the umbrella in my hands.

"Very true, *lopon*," said grandpa without looking at the man in red robes and continued to stitch up the tear in the garment.

"I think a *nyendu* like this will make my life much easier to live," the *Dorji lopon* said finally with the hope that my grandpa might offer the umbrella to him since grandpa was a very religious man, and he, as the *Dorji Lopon*, was well respected and a highly learned practitioner of Buddhism.

To this grandpa's forehead was an ocean of wrinkles. It looked like grandpa understood that the *Dorji Lopon* was trying to lure away the umbrella from him.

"I think so too, *lopon*," countered grandpa to my surprise. "How I wish the colour of this *nyendu* was red or orange instead of being black so that I could have offered it to you. I would have been most happy to offer this priceless possession of mine to you. But you will agree with me that black is not a colour for a revered religious personnel like yourself," added grandpa smartly to my utmost relief.

"Very true, *Maymay* Wamla. Very true indeed," agreed the *Dorji Lopon* half-heartedly, and walked away.

Well, yet again the umbrella was saved. There was no telling that grandpa would part with his umbrella so easily. He was going to keep it for himself at all cost.

*Maymay* Wamla took the umbrella wherever he went. He used it all the year round- in rain and in sun and even when there was neither of them. However, as time went by the umbrella began to break down gradually. The black cotton cloth tore up time and again, and grandpa patched it up repeatedly. Initially, he searched the house inside out for a piece of cloth that looked at least almost like that of the umbrella's. As the patching became more frequent, he patched up the torn umbrella with whatever cloth pieces he could lay his hands on. That in fact gave the umbrella a facelift. At least I thought so. I really liked the colourful patches on the umbrella. However, after grandpa had already patched and re-patched the umbrella about a dozen times, even the iron rods that acted as the pillars of the umbrella by holding the cotton cloth together began to give way. Again, initially he tied up the broken parts together with strong fibres from daphne or nettle plants. Later as the severity of the breakage intensified, he replaced them with canes that were strengthened by smoking them on the oven. He used most of the salvaged iron rods to make needles to sew leather bags and shoes, and some of them to make darts for me. Finally, when the canes broke down as well, he stripped the umbrella naked. "This is still good," he said, slashing the air with the cane that had an iron helmet and a hooked leg. "It will make a good walking stick for me. I need one for my bad legs anyway," he added with a chuckle.

By then, the umbrella had been in Khema for roughly a year. And, that year while other men and women left for Gudama, my grandpa did not. "I am too old to make such a journey anymore," he confided in me. "Your mother will have to replace me now," he added sadly.

Then, when my mother and the other travellers to Gudama came back from the trip, almost everyone had brought home a black umbrella. Besides bringing one for herself, my mother had brought one for me too. And, the village was full of black umbrellas that year.

Let's get back to my grandpa's umbrella again. Well, the old cane served faithfully as my grandpa's walking stick for as long as it could. Finally, some kind of an insect- I think it looked like a small troublesome wasp- made a hole in it one day against grandpa's knowledge and approval. Then, one fateful day the poor cane broke in half as grandpa tried to stand up by supporting on it. "There goes my faithful stick!" was grandpa's dismal remark. "It sure served me more than triple it's market price," he added sadly but fully satisfied with the stick's long and tiresome tenure firstly as the main part of his umbrella and then as a walking stick. He stared at the broken cane for a long time. Then, he summoned my mother and said, "Kezang, please do not burn it. Put it in the attic and let it rest there."

Soon after, my parents and I left home, and settled down in Thimphu. There I went to school, grew up into a man and found a job. Then, twenty-four years later I paid a visit to my birthplace that I had left behind and never turned back since the age of eleven. When I reached home, I witnessed that there was almost nothing left of my birthplace. Everything had changed. Un umbrella was nothing special in the village anymore. The village folks had sports wristwatches, dark sunglasses, cowboy hats and designer shoes. They were also expecting to be able to watch television soon since the silver coloured electric poles have already been installed in the next village that was only about five kilometres away. Everything that I remembered of my birthplace, except the mountain ranges and the small stream, was gone. Even the very house where my grandpa had lured me into keeping quiet by giving me candies have been relocated and rebuilt with no resemblance to the original one at all. I felt as if I was in a completely new place. If our old house had still been standing, I would have loved to search the attic for my grandpa's broken cane. But then, that was not possible anymore. Therefore, I left the village the very next day with a heavy heart. Nevertheless, I learned one of the biggest lessons of my life: never be away from what and whom you love for too long. If you did, much as you may love or remember them, they may not be there when you get back. And you may be left with nothing but some memories from a distant past.

***

# *Samphel's pride and woes*

Uncle Tobgay was my mother's 32 year-old only brother, a bachelor who had sworn never to get married. He dedicated his life in supporting his aged mother, widowed elder sister and his only nephew. The village folks called him Uncle *Tshongpa*- 'uncle' after me, but than again, even my mother addressed him uncle, and till I was eight, I always thought that my uncle was my mother's uncle too. He would make at least three trips a year to Gudama, an Indian town on the Indo-Bhutanese border. There he would barter hand-woven garments, bee wax, walnuts and pig-tail-hair with cotton, wool and silk yarns, salt, kerosene, cloth, dry fish, rubber shoes, sandals, tea, sugar and a score of varied other goods that his experiences over the years told him are in high demand back home. He would pack them all up firm and good, load them up on the backs of half a dozen ponies, and start the long journey home.

Uncle Tobgay's every departure to Gudama would always be followed by my consistent daily inquiry of his return from my mother. Since I knew how to count till 20 only, my mother would initially tell me that he would be back after 20 days. Then, after she had already told me the same thing for 20 days, the real countdown would begin, and I would be the happiest boy in the whole village. I would go around and 'show-off' my uncle's return to every single child in the village. And, every kid in the village would willingly share the peaches, pears, dried beef, beaten maize, and dry fried rice their mothers filled up their small pouches with when they came out to play with other kids. Of course, there were always some kids who wouldn't want to share their riches with me, but I would always know how to lure them into parting a portion of what they had. All I had to utter was, "Uncle Tobgay will be back tomorrow, and he will be bringing me candies and balloons." And the spell never failed.

At least two days before uncle's arrival, my mother would distil some wine, and store it in my late grand father's favourite short cylindrical wooden container with silver linings and gold curving. She would even shine the gold curving on the container with a piece of clean white cotton rug.

'This is how your uncle wants his wine and container' she would say with a sense of satisfaction after she had removed the last particle of dirt from it.

Uncle's first night at home after every trip always started with a ceremonial reception wine followed by a sumptuous dinner composed of dried beef and pork with potatoes and red chillies, fried cheese and bamboo shoot soup prepared with mother's 30 years' experience in cooking. I would be sitting right beside my uncle. After dinner, some relatives and friends would drop by with long cylindrical bamboo containers full of wine and sit around him like a flock of vultures eagerly waiting for their leader to finish partaking his share from a carcass of horse. And, uncle would begin the tales of his latest adventures. I would be sitting beside him, my neck craned and staring into his face to pick up every detail of the tale. He would be stroking my dust and lice ridden hair every now and than with his big callused hand in synchrony with the tales of his journey. And, the tales would go on late into the night and early into the next day till all the long bamboo containers were emptied, and his own wine container emptied and refilled half a dozen times by my mother. The house would be filled with *Paaaah*, *Zaaie* and *Waaie* of surprises and admiration of uncle's tales from the audience. And, I would be reassured that my uncle was truly the village's hero. I would be eventually laying in his lap and dozing off. And in my sleep, I would be Uncle *Tshongpa* myself on a journey to a distant land at the head of a few 20s of ponies.

Uncle's first day after arrival would always begin with a cup of wine served by my mother from his favourite wine container. When I looked at him curiously, he would try to explain his early morning drinking habit to me. "This is to drive away last night's ghosts from my body." Then, he would stroke my head again with his heavy hand and say, "Do not do this when you are a big boy, Samphel."

And, that would be just about enough for him to unleash the master big mouth in me. I would be talking to him and mother and grandmother and myself and Dungkarmo the cow, and Baytu the dog, and Mindula the horse, and Takarmo the cat and...till I fell asleep on his lap again that night.

Well, after the wine and a breakfast of millet dough with buttermilk, fresh cow's butter, potato curry and salted butter tea, uncle would unpack loads and loads of things. After every load had been unpacked, the gift distribution, the most waited session, would begin. I would be the first person to get the gift, followed by mother, grandmother and other relatives. He would also bring a slab of dried tealeaves, some betel nut and some dried

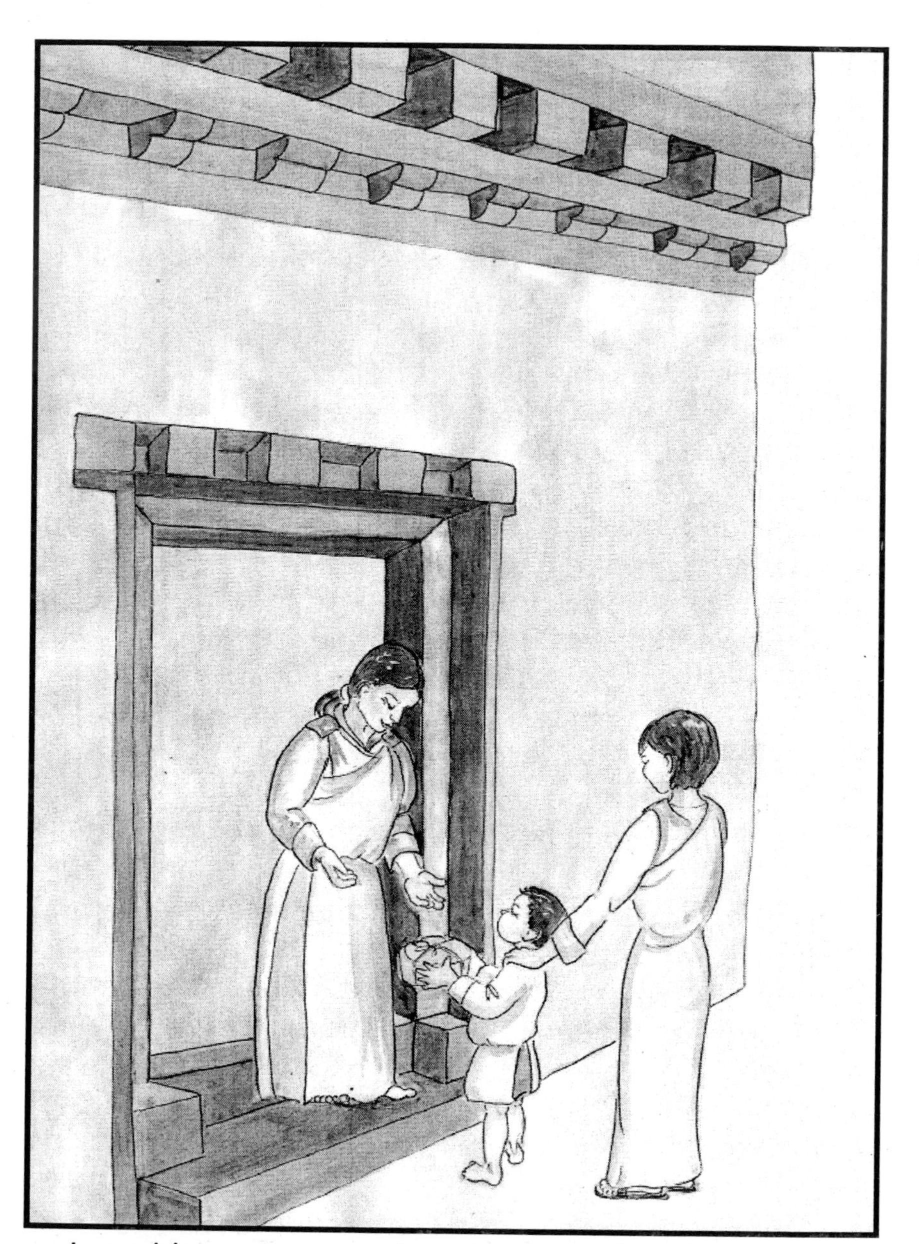

... I would crana my neck and repeat the messages at the top of my voice.

fish for every household in the village. My mother and I would go from door to door to deliver the gifts.

"Uncle sends this humble gift with his apologies that he couldn't bring more," my mother would say every time someone opened the door.

"Oh! He shouldn't have. It's not possible that he brings gifts every time he goes to Gudama. Would you please, thank him for me," the recipient would counter simultaneously receiving the gift.

After we had visited a few households, I would insist my mother that I will deliver uncle's message. And right after someone had opened the door, I would crane my neck and repeat the message at the top of my voice. My mother and the recipient of the gift would laugh their heads off, and I would blush.

"You did it very well there," mother would say as she ushered me by holding me by my hand to the next house.

"I can do even better at the next house," I would declare with confidence.

And, my mother would sweep me off my feet and kiss me on my red cheeks.

By the time my mother and I had delivered all the gifts, uncle would have already finished his part of the job. He would have already put aside enough quantities of cotton, wool and silk yarns for my mother to weave embroidered garments, salt, sugar, tea and dry fish for the family to last till his next return trip from Gudama, plain white cotton cloth for the twelve flag poles outside our house and wind-horses on the hillocks far north of our village, one fourth of his remaining goods put aside to be exchanged with rice, butter, cheese and meat for the family; that one fourth, he would consider as his net profit from the trip. After all things have been sorted out to his heart's content, as usual he would tell my very approving mother and grandmother that he would barter the rest with hand-woven garments, walnuts, bee wax, and pig tail hair again.

"After all, the business must go on," he would say with a chuckle and raised eyebrows, and even the village's deaf and the dumb could make out from the expression on his face that Uncle *Tshongpa* was happy with the prospect of his business.

Come the second day, and I would always wake up to see my uncle sitting in the middle of many 20s of things, and almost the entire village folks tugged up inside our small house. And still tugged up in my blanket, my eyes would traverse from uncle to the people in the house and the traffic at the door, and I would be lost for a moment or two to the humble-bumble of the crowd and in a thought of my own. I would always imagine myself in uncle's present 'throne' in the middle of many more 20s of things and many more 20s of people. And as usual, my uncle would walk over to my bed, and say '*Wai*, my *prince* is up' and rescue me out of the bed and curl me up in between his big masculine arms that felt as soft as the wool on a lamb's skin. Everybody would look at my uncle dressing me up in the new cotton *gho* and the gumboot he had brought for me.

"Such love for your nephew, Uncle *Tshongpa!*" the people around him would exclaim with envy.

"Samphel is my Prince," uncle would say with unhidden pride.

And, my red cheeks would redden even more from blushing with the added attention from the crowd while in a corner near the chimney, bent over a shimmering pot of maize powder porridge, my mother would acknowledge that I was a lucky boy, and wipe a drop of tear from the corner of her eyes with the back of her soot laden hand.

When I was five, uncle admitted me in the village's school for lay monks. Soon after, he left home for Gudama again at the head of half a dozen ponies as usual. And, the very next day I started counting the days of his return again. One night on the second half of 20 days, we heard a horse neighing outside our house.

"Mindula!" my mother exclaimed in surprise. She lit a pinewood flint in a flash and ran outside. "It is Mindula, *ama*! It is Mindula!" she shouted excitedly when she was outside.

And, I ran out of the house calling out, "Uncle, uncle" at the top of my voice.

"But... he is alone" mother gasped.

Mindula, uncle's favourite horse was surely standing outside alone.

When my mother saw me drowning in disappointment, she held my hand and said, "Uncle must have sent Mindula ahead to inform us of his arrival. Let's go inside and wait."

Later, when my mother went out to feed Mindula with un-husked rice and maize, my grandmother put her fragile hand on my head and double assured me that uncle will be home any moment. Just then, my mother walked in and sat beside grandmother, her face drained of blood. "Mindula is not eating," she said after a long time.

And, the long wait began. Uncle did not arrive.

Next morning while going to school, I saw Mindula still standing outside the house. As I walked by, something deep onside of me told me to stop. And, as I stood still, Mindula trotted towards me and muzzled me gently. Then, just as I was reaching out to stroke his forehead, he slumped to the ground in a slow motion. Nervously, I took a closer look at him, and then I realised how lean and thin he had grown. I bent over him, and stroked his forehead with utmost sympathy. He did not move. Mindula was dead.

I continued the countdown again. I counted the days over and over again. At the school I was promoted from *Ka, Kha, Ga,* and *Nga* to *Shonlob*, then to *Tshidue*, to *Dorchoed* and to *Digsha* and finally to *Shaju* but my uncle still did not return from Gudama. My mother cooked ground maize more often than usual. The menu at breakfast was always the same- maize powder porridge. There was not even a scent of dry fish in the house. The holes in my gumboot either kept on becoming bigger or multiplied in numbers till finally I had to part with it and walk barefooted. My two plain cotton *gho*s had already returned to mother earth while the last one already had a few multicoloured patches on it. My mother and I did not go door to door to deliver uncle's gifts anymore. Instead, we received gifts from other *Tshongpa*s. My spell to lure other village children into sharing their riches with me did not work anymore. My mother grew paler and leaner by the day, and the numbers of grey hair on her head kept on doubling by the day till her head was as grey as her mother's. My grandmother's gentle sobs changed to pathetic cries. Finally, she started running around naked, and eventually jumped from the roof of our house and never moved again. And, I counted many 20s of 20s of days till I could finally count till 100 over and over again. However, my uncle still did not come home. I would still tell my mother and everybody in the village that my uncle would be home any moment. But my uncle still did not come home.

Then, one day, my teacher at the school summoned me to his room. "Samphel, I know how much you want your uncle to come home," he said carefully. "Everyone including me in the village also know how much you love your uncle and how much he loved you." Then, he wore an uneasy look on his face, took a deep breath and said, "But I am sorry to tell you that your uncle will not be coming home anymore. You are old enough now. You must understand that certain things that happen in life cannot be undone once they have already happened. Your uncle disappeared in Gudama five years ago. Much as we have tried to find his body, we couldn't. And knowing how much you loved him, no one could tell you the truth till now. Now, you must be brave and accept this fact, but always remember that your uncle is always with you. I know he is. I can see him in you."

***

# *The avenger's return*

It was almost midnight. The residents of the small village of Khoma, with 18 houses clustered together in the narrow valley on the banks of the Khomachu River, slumbered peacefully after a hard day's work. The full moon shone shyly half hiding behind a cluster of dark clouds that cast ghostly shadows over half the village. A rooster crowed urgently from beneath the sandalwood-shingling roof of Jangchu's house, trying to break the silence of the night; but no other roosters headed the solitary call. A lonely jackal half-heartedly climbed a rock on the top of a nearby hillock and howled at the moon as though holding onto the tradition of a long tiresome vengeance against the moon. The village dogs barked at the jackal in unison. But still no man, woman or child stirred from his or her balmy bed. After all, this was the paddy harvest season, and everyone deserved to be having a good sleep at this time of the night. Yes, it was an autumn midnight.

Then, just as the dogs had started to lie down after having scared away the lonely jackal, the earth beneath their bare bellies started to tremble momentarily. And, even before they could open their mouths to let out their cries of fear to calm their nervous brains and fast throbbing hearts, silence ruled again, except for the rattling of some dry leaves on the almost naked peach trees in the cold mild breeze of the night. Then, suddenly the earth started to tremble again, stronger and stronger with every passing heartbeat, making the dogs cry helplessly and run hither and thither. The horses in the stables neighed and struggled at the ropes on their necks while the cattle in the cowsheds bayed helplessly trying to free themselves from whatever they have been tethered to. The chickens chipped and cocked noisily as they were shaken off their perches in their sleep.

By the time the residents of Khoma were on their feet, every pillar in their houses were swaying from side to side and every utensil on their kitchen shelves were crashing down on the wooden floors below. Mothers tried to calm down their crying babies and the grandparents fumbled for prayers and called to their guardian deities for help while the fathers and every able bodied men in the village tried to guide their women, children and kith and kin to safety. Some elderly people clung on to whatever they could grab and declined to move out of their houses, declaring that they would go down with their homes. Most residents ran frantically out of their houses, with their wives or children, parents, friends, relatives or whatever dearly belongings they could grab. Some were dragging people or things while others were carrying the same. Some were just running away from their rattling, cracking, quaking and swaying houses for their own lives in whichever directions their legs carried them. The village's air was filled with a cacophony of the cries of despair, cries for help, cries of terror, calls for lost relatives, screams of fright, prayers of refuge, thuds of running people and animals, noises of frightened animals, and a dozen other noises. The narrow footpaths in between the clustered houses were jammed with people, pigs, horses and cattle of every sex and age moving in no common direction. Then, suddenly the earth stopped trembling altogether, and the only noises in the village were those of the residents of the village. And, every man and animal alike stood still as if they had been dumbfounded and pinned to the very ground they were standing on. And silence reigned in the village again.

"People, calm down and slowly walk towards the archery ground," instructed Karma, the village headman at the top of his voice. "Do not return to your houses till I say so. The earthquake may return any moment," he warned.

All the nervous and terrified residents made their way to the archery ground that was about 300 yards from the periphery of the clustered houses. They waited there until the fifth crow of the cock but the earthquake did not return, and no lives or properties except for some broken utensils were lost that night.

Two days after the quake, Gyeltshen and his wife's day started like any other day. At the first crow of the village's lead rooster, Gyeltshen's wife busied herself in the kitchen preparing a breakfast of rice, chilly salad and salted butter tea for the workers that her family had hired for the day to harvest their paddy. Gyeltshen joined his wife only when all the village's roosters had crowed at least once after the lead rooster. Then, he began to churn the previous two-day's collection of milk from his seven milking cows. When dawn was just about to announce the start of a new day, his wife was already at the window calling out each and every worker that Gyeltshen had hired for the day by their names and asking them to come for breakfast. As her shrill voice filled up the village, every hired hand responded with a '*Ya, ya,* I am coming.'

By then, Gyeltshen had already finished churning milk and had separated the butter from the buttermilk. He was offering a small piece of fresh butter to the guardian deities and his family's snake deity with the prayers to bless his family with more milk and to protect his cattle from diseases and predators. While saying the prayers, he pasted three small balls of butter on one of the main pillars of the house with his thumb and threw another into the fire in the oven. Then, he put aside three fist-full-lumps of butter in a circular bamboo basket with lid for his three kids, and saved the rest in a wooden butter container. He also put aside a wooden bucket full of buttermilk for the workers and transferred the rest into a brass cauldron. He put the brass cauldron full of buttermilk on the live oven to make cheese. By the time he was filtering cheese with a bamboo mesh filter, his hired workers started to come in one by one and sit in the kitchen for breakfast. After the last worker from Berpa, a village half way up the mountain on the other side of the river, has arrived Gyeltshen's wife served them a hearty breakfast followed by some local wine.

Although two days had gone by since the earthquake, the incident was still on everyone's lips from breakfast and way into the ordeals of paddy harvest. And to everyone's surprise, the neighbouring villages of Khoma had not had even the slightest movement of the earth that night. And everyone- young and old- agreed that such an isolated earthquake had neither occurred in their lifetimes nor during their forefathers'.

At noon, Gyeltshen's wife arrived at the edge of the paddy field with a bamboo basket full of packed lunch on her back and a wooden bucket full of buttermilk in her right hand. She put down the wooden bucket carefully on a flat rock in the middle of a small patch of flat open grassland in a thicket of dogweed near her paddy field. She sat down carefully near the rock, balanced the bamboo basket on her back on the ground and took off the strap of the basket from her shoulders. Then, she walked over to the edge of the grassland, and called out to the workers to break for lunch.

Then, just as the workers sat down around Gyeltshen's wife for lunch, they heard a loud rambling noise coming from Khoma. As all eyes fell on the village, they saw Gyeltshen's house falling apart in a cloud of dust. Everyone rushed to the site, with terror clear in their faces as they anticipated all the other houses to fall apart as well. However, no other houses fell apart. Only that of Gyeltshen's! Yes, only Gyeltshen's ten-month old house, the second largest in the village that was located in the centre of the village. "A single whirlpool of dust laden wind blew towards the village from the west, passed over the houses on the way, smashed against Gyeltshen's house, fell it, and disappeared as quickly as it came," reported an eyewitness.

Gyeltshen's three children had escaped the tragedy since they were playing with their playmates at a distance from their house when the storm struck their house. However, Gyeltshen's mother in-law's body had to be dug up from under the debris of the dilapidated building. As the neighbours helped Gyeltshen dig up what was left of his properties, his weeping wife blamed him for the tragedy. "Gyeltshen, you should have known better than to quarrel with a *Nyenpa*'s son. If you had but just turned the other cheek that day, my mother would be alive now! If you had just walked away from Dorji that day, our house would still be standing and my mother would still be alive," repented the mourning lady.

And Gyeltshen and all his neighbours knew that his wife meant it well. Gyeltshen should have known better.

Tashi, the astrologer- so was he addressed by people far and near, although behind his back most people called him the *Nyenpa*, literally meaning 'the bad one' but the very name or designation or, if you wish, profession simply means 'the one who casts evil or bad spells on others or the one who practised the witchcraft- was a happy man today. Gyeltshen was in a pathetic condition. Gyeltshen has lost his home, and is currently putting up with a relative sympathiser.

"I can destroy that home too if I want to," Tashi thought with a broad smile on his face. "But Tandin and his family has done me no harm," he reasoned against his evil temptations. "Besides, Gyeltshen still has a funeral to prepare." He chuckles as he partakes a cup of hot salted butter tea, sitting in his altar room. "That will teach Gyeltshen and anyone who dares to mess up with me or my son not to try to act smart."

Just then Dorji, Tashi's only son dashes into the altar room. "Father... father, I just heard that Gyeltshen...."

"I know." Tashi said coldly as Dorji was trying to catch his breath. "He won't beat you up again. He wouldn't dare."

"You mean you...."

"He has been punished. That is all you need to know," countered Tashi, his voice deep and his unspoken message clear in his cold eyes.

Dorji knew his father well enough to try to pursue the conversation any further. Most of all, he knew his father's trade well. As his father had said, it was enough that Gyeltshen has been punished for beating him up in the public just because he teased Gyeltshen's teenage sister. So, he quietly walked away out of the room.

After his son has left the room, Tashi sipped his tea again and again, more to distract himself from his conscience than for want of drinking the tea. Then, suddenly as the loneliness blanketed him, faces from times long gone flashed in his head. The memories of the cries of woes, the laughter of joys, the heartaches of departing and the smiles of welcome all flashed in his tired brains. He shook his head, shut his eyes tight and opened them wide again trying to free himself from the flashbacks of his life from long ago. Then, as he took a big gulp of the salted tea again, he heard his wife's sweet voice at a distance. "Tashi, you are a heavy man!" He shook his head again trying desperately to wave way the memories. "Tashi, please do something. This *lama* is trying to drag me away!" he heard his dying wife say. Only this time the scene that flashed in his head was from that of his second wife dying in her bed eighteen years ago. Then, there were others and many more things and happenings that kept his mind preoccupied continuously against his will. Finally, alone in the altar room, he wished that such flashbacks did not come to him. At last, as he panted and sweated from the heartaches of his days gone by, he desperately wished he was dead.

Well, a person who did not notice the traumas that sixty-nine year old Tashi was going through would have thought Tashi's life was not really bad. After all, he was wealthy and one of the most respected men in the whole of Kurtoe. However, Tashi had his own reasons for not being able to afford the luxuries of his well-accumulated wealth and hard earned respect. He was no more a normal member of the society but a *Nyenpa* who was self-conscious enough but had either landed up doing all the wrong things and or does all the immoral things and regrets them way after it was all too late.

When Tashi was a kid, his parents had had to work their bone marrow dry in others' fields trying to sustain their family. However, they had never had enough. He and his six brothers and sisters were brought up in rags. The only times they partook a meal of pure rice were on the New Year's day and the Day of the Meeting of the Nine Evils. For the other 362 days, they had to do with mostly porridge or dough of maize or millet powder day in and day out. Most of their neighbours would sympathise his family for their poverty and would give them their leftover food and worn-out cloths while others would either bully or insult them.

When he was fifteen, Kencho Tshering, the village's most powerful and wealthy man had beaten up his father badly for not being able to repay a loan of one hundred *dreys* of maize. His father had succumbed to the beatings a few days later leaving behind his mother a widow with seven children to feed and cloth. His mother was a simpleton and one of the most timid ladies in the village. She was afraid of even a leach or a mouse. So, it had been easy for his father's murderers to hush her up, through threats, against reporting the case to the Governor. Besides, even the village headman and the village elders had taken sides with Kencho Tshering, and settled the case for just two silver coins. Tashi being the eldest child had tried to get even with his father's murderer by attacking him with a dragger single-handed, but Kencho

Tshering and his four able-bodied sons had almost taken his soul away by beating him up. They had also threatened to kill him if he did not leave the village for good. Tashi had had no choice but to leave his newly widowed mother with six siblings and run for his life. His mother had given him the two silver coins and begged him never to return to the village until his enemies were all dead.

Tashi had wandered from place to place doing odd jobs for almost five years. Then, he had finally settled down in the land of the *Brokpa*s. There he had met Chimi the eldest of the three daughters of a wealthy *Brokpa* who owned more than a hundred yaks and almost a quarter of the village's wheat and barley fields. All his in-laws had liked and respected him for his hard work. His in-laws would even send one of their servants with at least five horse-loads of grains, meat, butter, cheese and cloths for his family back home once every year, although his own village was more than a week's journey. It had not been until about two years later that he had finally found out that his father in-law was the best *Nyenpa* in the whole of the *Brokpa* land. Nevertheless, it was then said that the man never used his powers for his own benefits. He would only use the power to either undo a wrong done by other *Nyenpa*s or to deliver justice on request by a helpless person.

One day, while Tashi and his wife were on their way to their yakshed to deliver ration for their yak herders, Chimi had asked, "You never told me anything about your father. Where is he? What does he do?" taking Tashi by surprise.

He had halted in his stride and looked blankly into her eyes for a long time as his memories had taken him back to the days when his father's life was ended by Kencho Tshering's beatings. As he was lost in the gloomy memories of his recent past, Chimi had held his hand, squeezed it tight and sat down on the flat rock by the roadside, and pulled him down gently onto her own lap.

"Tell me about him," she had insisted. "Please tell me," she had urged in her sweet seductive voice.

"He is dead," he had replied coldly, his eyes fixed on the dusty mule track and his body rigid as the very mountain they were on. "He was murdered," he had added after a long silence and had slowly unfolded the story to her.

After he had finished narrating the story of his father's tragic death, he had said, "Let us get going or we will never make it to the shed," trying to swallow the bitter gall.

Chimi had been dumbfounded for a while, and then she had taken a deep breath as he had gently helped her up on her feet. "Tell me more about your life. You have never told me how you happened to come to our village," she had said.

She had stood still and stumped her feet gently on the ground a couple of times trying to enhance the blood flow in her numb legs. "You are a heavy man, Tashi!" Chimi had teased him.

Then, as the two were driving their ponies through the rocky pass on the summit of a mountain, Tashi had unfolded the rest of his life story. By the time they had descended the mountain and were half way to the pinnacle of another, Tashi had shared all his secrets with his wife. "Those five years were very hard times for me, even harder than my childhood. But what are those times as compared to my father's death in the hands of that rich, powerful and highly influential family!" he had remarked with remorse. "And then I got lucky and met you, the most beautiful and kind hearted person I have ever met in my life."

"Let's take another rest," she had suggested. Then, she had swiftly but gently and almost tiptoeing ran to the second horse in the procession. She had caught it by its reins and whistled softly as she fumbled into a bamboo basket on its back. Within seconds, she had taken out a small cylindrical bamboo container of local wine. Then she had given the horse two gentle pats on its neck, backed off and blew two sharp coherent whistles through her crocked index finger tugged into her mouth. As the horses moved on, she had ran back to Tashi who had by then laid down on his back on a carpet of primulas in bloom and was staring into the sky at a cluster of cumulus cloud being gently blown away by the wind. Chimi had stood over him and looked down into his face with a broad beautiful smile that could have stolen even her own murderer's heart. Her black cascade of silky hair had fluttered like a wind-horse flag in a gentle gust of wind. Then, as she gaily giggled and sat down beside him and started to fill a maple cup with wine, he had realised for the hundredth time how desperately loveable and perfectly beautiful his wife was. And his sorrows had been momentarily blown away by the chilling alpine wind again.

"Alright, my hero, get up and warm up yourself with this," she had said handing over the cup of wine to him.

"As long as you are beside me, I will always be warm, my dear. Not even all the ice and the snow in the mountains can cool me down," he had assured her as genuinely as possible.

And, as the blush on her perfectly blended complexion on her perfectly nurtured face had made her look even more beautiful, he had pasted a pinch of black soil on her cheek.

"Let no eyes fall on my wife, the most beautiful lady in all of the *Brokpa* land and beyond," he had prayed jokily.

And the two had gotten lost in one another's arms on a carpet of primulas.

The next day as the couple were walking down a rocky crop of granite and marble on the face of a dead volcanic mountain, Chimi had said, "You told me about your father yesterday. Now I will tell you a few things that you may not be aware of about my father."

As he listened on, she unfolded her father's tale as if reading out a well-written text.

Her father was a reincarnate of a Tibetan *lama*. Upon recognition by a group of Tibetan *lama*s at the age of four, he had been taken to Kham in Tibet and educated under the strict guidance of a group of *lama*s. By the time he was twenty-four years of age, he had miraculously mastered all the teachings and dogma of the Gelugpa sect. Then, as he was secretly mastering the doctrines of the Nyengmapa sect from a close Nyengmapa *lama*, one of his sworn Gelugpa *lama* rival who had been trying to overthrow him from his monastery in Khamtoe, had learned of his secret and had reported against him. The council of regents of his monastery headed by his rival had then banished him from Kham. Then, as he had tried to settle down in the province of Ling, his rivals had tried to assassinate him secretly through a gang of hired bandits. Her father had had no choice but to use his well mastered powers of the *Thu* to defend himself and his followers. At the casting of a spell by her father, all the bandits had been engulfed by a miraculous storm of fire as they were approaching his newly constructed monastery under the cover of darkness.

A few days later, his rivals had taken him to the court of the province's Governor accusing him of being a black magician, and had demanded the Governor to execute him publicly. On the very night the verdict was delivered, he cast a spell again to put his foes into deep slumber. As the governor imprisoned him and waited for Lhasa's approval of his execution, he had again used his powers. Under his spell everyone in the fortress, including the Governor had floated away into a deep slumber for a whole day and a whole night. Then, he had walked away from the fortress's prison in broad daylight.

He had had neither a horse nor any companion, and not even a handful of wheat flour with him when he had fled from Tibet. However, he had managed to travel all the way across the barren Tibetan plateau and the dreaded snow-capped mountains north of Bhutan and home safely with neither a scratch on his body nor a drop of sweat on his forehead. By then, he had been gone from home for thirty-one years. He had never related to anybody the secrets of how he had miraculously survived the tedious and near to impossible journey alone. Ever since he had been practising the dogma of Nyengmapa although almost all the people in the *Brokpa* land were Gelugpas. Nevertheless, he would preach Gelugpa to any devotee who approached him and requested for his teachings.

However, he had become a changed man. His experiences in Tibet and presumably the journey from Tibet to Bhutan seemed to have consumed all the compassion of a Bodhisattva in him. He had spent the next twenty-five years mastering and excelling himself in *Thu*, and fighting an evil war with his rivals in Kham. It was believed that he had taken the lives of all his rivals, including the conspirators in his monastery in Kham. He had also reduced the ancient monastery in Kham, which was his birthright, to dust using his *Thu*. And, for this he had been feared and officially disowned by the Gelugpa sect.

"One thing my father never learned is to forgive," Chimi had concluded sadly. "You better mind how you treat me, or you will have a piece of my father's wrath," she had teased him.

"Chimi, I want to get even with Kencho Tshering," Tashi had said coldly. "Do you reckon that your father will teach me the *nyen*?" he had asked without a second thought.

"Tashi, what in the world are you talking about! No, I will not have you do this. Your father is already dead. Would taking revenge bring him back! No, Tashi. No. Don't even think of it," she had said getting hysterical.

" I must approach your father for help," he had declared.

"Tashi, you are a good man. You know that evil begets only evil. It is not for a mortal to punish a wrong doer. The Lord of the Judgement Day will deliver the justice!" she had tried to reason.

"If getting even with Kencho Tshering is the last thing I do, I will do it without remorse," Tashi had countered through gritting teeth.

And, Chimi had understood that nothing could subdue the fire of anger in her husband's heart.

The next day, Tashi had approached his father in-law, narrated his tale of misfortune, and begged him to teach him the *nyen*. "I will teach you the *nyen*. But you must promise me that you will use it only against those who had bestowed upon you great losses and pain," the father in-law had cautioned. "You must, however promise me that you will not take anybody's life, not even that of your greatest foe's. You will use it only to destroy their properties and inflect physical and mental pain on them, but not take their lives. And you will use it to defend yourself, your family and the helpless," he had insisted.

And, Tashi had readily given his word.

Tashi's father in-law had taught him the *nyen* for two years. Thereafter, on the advice of his teacher Tashi had meditated and practised the *nyen* for six months in a lonely hut in the mountains about three hours' journey from his wife's village. Then, he had worked in the barley and wheat fields for half a year and finally proposed to his father in-law that he be allowed to spend some time with the family's yak herd. After getting approval from his father in-law, he had cooed Chimi into staying back home, and had left for the yakshed alone. There he had taken every chance he had to cast the most powerful spells of destruction on his father's murder.

At around the same time, back at Tashi's birthplace, Wangdi who was half-heartedly herding a herd of cattle in a nearby forest had been in deep thought. "It's been about nine years since Tashi has left the village," he had been thinking. "Tashi's mother has been receiving five pony loads of goods every year from Tashi for the last three years, and again the same just a few days ago. Looks like Langamo's poor days are over. The things that Tashi sent her are enough to meet the needs of her family. Besides, people say that Tashi has also sent her six silver coins this time."

He had spared a deep sigh as he felt some kind of uneasiness build up inside of him. Just then, a deer's bark at a distance had distracted him for a while. He had reached out for his horn and blown it hard a couple of times. He knew that sometimes a deer barking the way it did that moment meant that a predator was lurking around. So, he had listened carefully, but the deer had stopped barking and his cattle had been grazing calmly. That indicated that there was no danger of the presence of a predator nearby. So, he had lain down on his back under the shade of a huge tree. Then, his mind had been preoccupied by the thoughts of Tashi again. "Tashi has become the talk of the village. Even a four-year-old kid in the village knows that Tashi has gotten married into a rich family in a distant land," he thought, his heart full of jealousy, and wishing that he was in Tashi's place. "That way I won't have to herd my father's cattle," he had said aloud as he pulled off a leach from his bare feet and threw it hard on a flat rock beside him full of vengence.

Then, as he felt something cold running down his feet, he had sat up beside the wriggling leach, pulled up his left feet onto his lap and wiped off the blood with a leaf. Then, he had plastered the small profusely bleeding wound with a pinch of black soil, and stared at the leach grudgingly, his anger clear in his bulging eyes. As the anger built up inside him, he had picked up the leach and smashed it hard on the rock with all his might. At the impact, Wangdi's blood had gushed out of the leach's mouth, and Wangdi had spared a smile of satisfaction. Still not satisfied with the way he has punished the leach, he had reached for a stick, picked up the leach, ran the stick down the leach's mouth and turned the leach inside out. Then, he had put it back on the rock making sure that the sun's rays fell directly on the leach. "This is what you get for sucking my blood, you wretched parasite," he had cursed through his trembling lips. "Now I will watch you die as the sun sucks you dry," he had added with immense sense of satisfaction at the way he was punishing the leach.

After a while the leach had stopped moving and had begun growing smaller in size as the sun drained away its body fluids. Then, the sky had suddenly grown dark. A lightening had flashed brightly blinding him momentarily. This had been followed by the loudest thunder he had ever heard in his life. And even as Wangdi was getting up on his feet, the sky had become clear again. The bright sun had shone as if the dark clouds that had darken the sky just a flash ago had just vanished as fast as they had gathered. Then, suddenly the sky had grown dark again, and the forest around him had swayed like a monk reading the *sutra*. As Wangdi was about to make a dash out of the forest, he had heard a storm headed towards him from the Northeast. He was frozen in his fears and had not been able to move. As he had looked on towards the approaching storm, a whirlpool of roaring and whistling storm had hit a gigantic tree about 100 yards from him. The tree had gone crashing down, taking down with it all the smaller trees in its way. The smaller trees in turn had taken down other trees of their own sizes and those smaller than themselves. Then, as the trees finally crashed onto the bamboo undergrowth below, the forest had been filled with a cacophony of crashes and baying of cattle. Then, instantly the forest had lit up again under the bright sun in the sapphire sky. And the only noises in the forest had been that of the baying cattle.

When Wangdi had run to the rescue of his cattle, what he saw had made him feel dizzy and weak in his legs. He had slumped onto a thicket of fern and lain there for a moment vomiting out whatever was in his vowels. After a while he had slowly walked to the site. At the site there had been at least 15 either dead or dying cattle lying around in the undergrowth of the forest beside or under the fallen trees. Some cattle had had their heads clear off their bodies as if chopped off by an expert swordsman. Some had been wriggling on their sides and kicking maliciously with unbearable pains. And the entire forest had been filled with sickening odour of cattle's blood and excreta.

Wangdi had run from one animal to the other like a man possessed. His mouth had been wide open and his eyes bulged so far out of their sockets as if they were about to fall off. Then Wangdi had looked at his blood soaked feet, gasped for air and ran out of the forest screaming at the top of his voice.

When Wangdi had reached the hilltop on the outskirts of his village, he had tried to call for help. However, he had noticed his house engulfed in a cloud of dust. There had also been a lot of people running around his house. So, he had decided against calling for help, and had rushed to his house as fast as he could. When he reached his house, he had seen his house falling apart like of mud-baked replica of a house forged by the untrained hands of a child at play under attack from a heavy shower of monsoon rain. Wangdi had frozen in his stride. When his mother noticed his presence behind the crowd, she had rushed to him and shook him awake.

"What is happening today!" he had exclaimed, his face drained of blood.

"I don't know, Wangdi. Our house started to tremble and fall apart for no reason at all," his mother had reported. Then, she had choked and broken down.

"There is nothing anybody can do now, Wangdi," one of his neighbours standing in front of him had remarked, "With the building falling apart at this rate, it would be dangerous to try to save what is inside."

"Initially we thought that there was an earthquake, but when we reached outside, there was nothing and still our house was trembling and falling apart," Rinchen the eldest son had said joining his mother and younger brother.

"Is our father and brother back from Autsho?" Wangdi had asked. Autsho was a small village about one and a half days' walk from Khoma.

"No, they will be here only by sunset this evening," Rinchen had replied.

"*Achey*, come with me. I have something to tell you," Wangdi had whispered, and led his elder brother away from the crowd.

After his wife and sons had told him everything, Kencho Tshering had remained dumbfounded for a long while.

"Did you say about 15 cows, Wangdi?" he had asked of his son after a long silence.

"Yes, but I don't know the exact number yet. There were calves and bulls as well," Wangdi had replied.

"And you have not been able to go back to the forest today!" Kencho had remarked.

"No, *apa*, we were all busy trying to recover what was left of our properties from the house," Rinchen had replied coming to Wangdi's rescue. "But we have already asked a few village men to help us tomorrow. We'll go to the forest tomorrow and...."

"Good. Rinchen, go to our village astrologer and tell him to come and see me immediately," the father had commanded without giving Rinchen the time to complete what he had to say. "And tell him that I want him to find out the cause of the day's tragedy so that he would know what things to bring along with him," Kencho Tshering had instructed his son.

As Rinchen was making his way to the door, his aunt had suggested that he take some tea fist. At this, Kencho had almost jumped up with anger. "The tea can wait but not what we must do, you fools," he had roared.

"We have just conducted a grand ritual to appease our guardian deities last month. I am sure that this can not be a punishment from them," Kencho's wife had remarked.

"I guess you are right. I get a feeling that this is the work of a *Nyenpa*," Kencho had said.

The astrologer had quietly unfolded an old worn-out scripture and read it to himself.

"Looks like it is the work of an evil spell caster," he had announced after having read about two pages of the scripture.

Then, he had neatly stacked up the scripture and wrapped it up with an equally worn-out piece of red cotton cloth.

"Anyway, let's see what the prayer beads say," he had added handing over his prayer bead to Kencho.

Kencho had received the prayer beads into the palm of both his hands, placed it over the smoky incense, put it on his head and murmured a silent prayer. Then, with the prayer beads still on his head, he had ran the thumbs and index finger along two opposite sides of an imaginary centre of the beads, held it firm and passed it to the astrologer. The astrologer had murmured a prayer and counted the beads in pairs, one from each side of the prayer bead.

"Yes, it says the same thing," the astrologer had concluded. "Do you want to find out who has cast the spell?" he had asked of Kencho.

"Please, *lopon tsipa*," Kencho had pleaded concurrently.

The astrologer had unfolded his scriptures again, fumbled for a certain page, looked at it for a while and announced, "The spell caster is from the Northwest of this village." Then, he had looked at the same page again for a long time and said, "He is in his twenties. He is tall and has a fair complexion. And looks like he had some kind of a dispute with you... I don't know what."

"I think I know who he is. I have just heard at Autsho about him and his family. I am sure that his father in-law is doing this for him," Kencho had concluded. "I want you to retaliate for me," he had commanded.

"But who do you think is that man. It would be dangerous for both of us to try to counteract the spell if his spell is stronger than mine," the astrologer had cautioned.

"I will give you a silver coin and a *Jatsham* if you do me the favour," Kencho had insisted.

"If you insist," the astrologer had agreed. "But I need additional six lay monks to help me," he had added.

"I will arrange everything, *lopon tsipa*. But when will you do it? I would appreciate if you could start right away," Kencho had said impatiently.

"There are a lot of arrangements to be made. I hope it will be agreeable to you if we do it tomorrow night. And in the mean time you can prepare for the ritual," the astrologer had suggested courteously.

Early next morning, Wangdi had led his three bothers and eight village hands to the forest, each with a large bamboo basket on his back. They had smelled flesh and blood a few hundred yards away. When they had reached the spot, they had seen at least two dozen wild dogs and a leopard, their faces smeared in blood, prowling all over the place. As the beasts sensed the presence of men, they had gnawed at the carcasses faster, growling and grunting aggressively. Then, the men had fumbled for stones underneath the black moist humus and had tried to shoo away the uninvited guests of leopard and wild dogs throwing a shower of fast moving stones at them. At that, only a hand full of small wild dogs had stopped eating and looked around nervously while the leopard and the big and fierce looking wild dogs had growled back and shown their white fangs sending a chill through the men's spines. As the men anticipated the approaching danger, they had thrown more and bigger stones at the beasts, shouting at the top of their voice. Then, slowly the beasts had backed off from the carcasses in front of them and dashed through the thick undergrowth of the forest. Wangdi and his team had thrown more stones and whatever they could lay their hands on after the animals and had made whatever noise they could to make sure that the animals were well off to a safe distance. After they had ascertained that they were safe from the wild animals, they had inspected the spot within a radius of about 100 yards. They had counted 20 heads, 11 of cows, 7 of calves and 2 of breeding bulls. At least a dozen giant trees had been brought down by the storm. But only in the area where Wangdi's cattle had been grazing. There had been no signs, what so ever of the fury of the storm around the rest of the forest.

Within just about four hours, the group had returned from the forest, their bamboo baskets full of meat.

"Is this all?" Kencho had asked taking a swift glance at the heap of meat outside his house.

"No, *apa*, there are still two loads left in the forest. *Achey* Rinchen and I will go back for them right away while the others dress the carcass to dry them," Wangdi had replied.

"This means that you were wrong last night!" Kencho had remarked optimistically thinking that 15 cattle would have yielded much more carcass.

"Yes, *apa*," Wangdi had replied. He had taken an awkward steep backward and had spared a long sheepish look at the people around him as if seeking for their help. After a long while, he had reported, "Only that it was more than 15. We have lost 20 of them, *apa*."

"The rest of the meat has been eaten up by wild animals," Rinchen had added finally coming to the rescue of his younger brother.

That had been followed by condolences and the tales of how they had driven away the beasts and the way the storm had brought about the tragedy to Kencho's cattle from the members of the group that had brought home the carcasses. Some had told Kencho that the guardian deity of the forest could have brought about the tragedy while others said that it could have been the doing of a *Nyenpa*.

At midnight after the residents of the village had all gone to bed, the astrologer had been busy with six other lay monks performing a ritual in the altar room of Kencho's new home. From time to time, the house had been filled with the eerie sound of a trumpet. This was followed by the cacophonic music from the beating of drums, clanging of cymbals, blowing of conch and clarinet and ringing of bell.

At exactly midnight, on the advice of the astrologer, the Altar Attendant had taken a mimic statue of a man out of the altar room and put it facing Northeast in the middle of the footpath outside the house. Moments after the Altar Attendant had returned to the altar room, a gust of wind had opened the main door, blown hard into the altar room that was across the first room from the main door, and blown out all the butter lamps in the room. Then, to the horror of everyone in the house, the house shook momentarily as if hit by an earthquake. Moments later, the statue that had been put outside the house a few minutes ago had appeared in front of the astrologer out of nowhere. As the statue had moved, as if it had a life of its own, on the small table in front of the astrologer, the terrified astrologer had backed off from the table and plastered himself against the wall. The other lay monks had ran out of the altar room screaming at the top of their voice. Then, when the statue had stopped moving, the astrologer had fumbled for his bag and dashed out of the room as well.

"That *Nyenpa* is too strong for me or anyone I know of. No one can help you now, *Apa* Kencho," the astrologer had warned as he hurried out of the house.

After that incident, Kencho Tshering had been doomed for life. Within six months, his wife, his four sons, his horses and even his chickens had fallen dead one after another as if they were all in a hurry to pay a visit to the Lord of Death. Kencho himself had turned a cripple who could not even go to the toilet without help. Later, when he heard from his village's traders who had been to the land of the *Brokpa* about Tashi having mastered the *nyen* from his father in-law, he had deeply regretted for what he had done to Tashi and his father. Then, he had devoted the rest of his life in chanting the sacred spells of Avalokitiswara to seek refuge in Him as well as to cleanse himself of his sins.

Back at the yakshed in the mountains of the land of the *Brokpas*, one day while Tashi was giving salt to his yak bulls, one of his father in-law's servants had visited him. "*Ama* Chimi asks you to come home right away," the man had said.

"Why? Is anything wrong?" Tashi had asked.

"I don't know, *lopon*. I was just instructed to convey this message to you," the messenger had replied.

Tashi had packed up and left for home in fear of the worst. When he reached home, he had rushed to Chimi who was breast-feeding his six moths old baby boy in the bedroom. "What have you been doing at the yakshed?" Chimi had asked of him as soon as he had entered the room.

"What else! Looking after the yaks, of course," Tashi had replied as a matter of fact.

"Don't you dare lie to me, Tashi," Chimi had fumed with anger.

"Lie to you? Of course, I won't lie to you. What is wrong with you? Why are you acting like this? Is this any way to greet your husband?" Tashi had exclaimed with surprise, sat beside her and reached for the baby.

"Don't you dare touch my baby, you murderer," Chimi had shouted turning away from him.

"What do you mean?

"You destroyed your old enemy, didn't you!" Chimi had accused.

Tashi who was lost for word had stared blankly at his wife.

"The horsemen who had been to your village arrived yesterday. They told me everything. So, don't you try to deny anything."

A long silence had followed.

"Chimi, please try to understand me. After all, this was why I learned the *nyen* from your father. Yes, to get even with my foes," Tashi had said trying to defend himself.

"But why did you have to kill five people? Why? Didn't you promise me and my father that you will never take a man's life?" Chimi had burst into tears.

"Yes, I did. But didn't they kill my father?" Tashi had argued.

"And you killed five of them! You are a murderer, Tashi. Murderer!" Chimi had screamed and clawed his face with her right hand while holding the baby in her left.

"Stop this madness, Chimi. Or else," Tashi had warned.

"What are you doing to do? Kill me too? I won't be surprised if you killed me and our baby as well, you murderer!" Chimi had screamed.

Then, as the anger pooled up in him, Tashi had slapped Chimi on her face and sent her and the baby down onto the floor. Just then, Chimi's parents had walked into the room.

"Did you hit my daughter, Tashi!" the old man had exclaimed in his cold and hoarse voice. "How dare you?"

Tashi had not moved at all. Nor had he uttered a word.

"And you have broken your promise too! I know everything about what you have been doing while at the yakshed," the father in-law had remarked, his voice full of loathing for Tashi.

"So what?" Tashi had challenged at last as his anger overtook his patience again. "So what if I have cast some evil spell and killed a few people. They were cruel to me, and they killed my father. You are a *Nyenpa* too. Don't tell me that you haven't killed a few people yourself!"

"Enough! I want you out of my house and out of my village right now," declared the old man. "And Chimi, you can do what you want to- stay with your parents or leave with Tashi. But I want Tashi out of my house and out of my village," he had roared.

"I can live with a father who is a *Nyenpa* but not a husband of the same kind. I won't have my husband turn my son into a murderer," Chimi had announced.

That was a long time back, recalls Tashi. After he was thrown out of his wife's house, he had rushed home to his mother. Now, here he was at fifty-six, rich and powerful, and respected and feared by all. But his success had not come cheap either. He had lost his mother,

... he found himself laying in Chimi's lap on a carpet of primulas...

brother and sisters, his second wife and three lovely children from her. His father in-law had never forgiven him, and taken the hatred towards him to his deathbed about fifteen years after Tashi had left the land of the *Brokpa*s. Tashi had never known if his own *nyen*, which he had no choice but to return to defend himself and his family, or the old age had killed the old man. Nevertheless, it was rumoured that it was the former that ended his father in-law's life. At fifty-six, Tashi did neither know how Chimi was doing nor did he try to find out about her and his son. He knew that she was as stubborn as her father was, and she would never have forgiven him either. Then, as he sipped his tea again, he felt the loneliness creeping up inside him.

A year later, Tashi was on his way to another village. As he rode his pony through a narrow track up a cliff, he heard a rumbling noise at a distance uphill. His pony stood still as if frozen by the chilling winds blowing from the northern snow-capped mountains. As he tried to make the pony move, he heard the rumbling noise drawing nearer and nearer. Suddenly the earth beneath him shook. Then, as he was getting down from the unmoving pony, he felt the sky above his head grow dark. And, suddenly tones of rock and earth fell on him, and carried him and his pony off the narrow track and down the cliff. As his limbs and head tore apart from his body and got scattered in the swift avalanche, he found himself laying in Chimi's lap on a carpet of primulas on a mountain in the land of the *Brokpa*s.

***

# *The clandestine foes*

In my village, one can never be too careful. No matter what, one could get kidnapped and hidden by so many things. Yes, things because they are not humans. They are either a *Tshen*, or a *Dredpo* or a *Dud*. This is why not many people dare to be or pass by alone in a number of places such as a particular forest, pass, cliff, deserted house or houses, or even a particular rock or tree. Should circumstances necessitate one to visit or pass such a particular place or thing, one always does it by the light of the day, seldom at night, and preferably with company. And of course, there are the ghosts of all kinds who either harm you or possess you.

Although I was always afraid of getting kidnapped by either a *Tshen* or a *Dredpo* when I was a kid since I had to frequent their habitats while herding cattle, I was never kidnapped. But, hush! The elders say that one must never ever say things like 'I was never kidnapped' or 'I have never seen a ghost' or 'This or that has never happened to me.' They say that if one said such a thing, he or she will be doomed to experience that very thing. But I have no choice here since what I have just said has a lot of relevance (I think!) to a part of what I am going to narrate to you about. Besides, I cannot help but share with you my own experience first.

When I was eight, my parents' three horses did not come home for three nights in a row.

"They must have sneaked away to Binakhar," my father said after my family members have had a long 'guess work' of where the horses could be at that moment.

Now, Binakhar was our village's community grazing land. It was about three hours' walk uphill from our village. It had many hundreds of acres of grassland that was enough to sustain all the cattle of our village for two months a year. A dense forest of gigantic sub-temperate evergreen trees that tried to touch the skies and all sorts of bamboo specie- tall, short, thick, and thin, with thorns and without thorns- separated our village from Binakhar. I never liked the forest. It was too dark, too deep, and really creepy. Besides, it had wild animals of all kinds that made equally scary noises. However, I loved Binakhar then because the first and the last time I had been there, it was but full of green grasses and red and white of wild strawberry fruits and flowers. I had had a good time then.

"If you go to Binakhar, I would also like to come along with you, *apa*," I volunteered hastily as my mouth began to water at the thought of the strawberries.

"No, you can't go with *apa*," objected my mother. "It is not safe at this time of the year," she added hesitantly.

"Come now, *ama*! Don't be timid. Let Pema go with me if he wants to," countered my father.

"But, you know that nobody is supposed to enter Binakhar at this time of the year!" protested my mother.

" Don't worry. We will not make any noise there," he reassured mother. "And I'll keep Pema under my nose at all times," he promised to my relief.

Well, it was only about three years later that I could fully understand why my mother was reluctant in letting me accompany my father to Binakhar that day. That day had been the twenty-first day of the third month of the lunar calendar, and like in any other year, no man was supposed to visit Binakhar at that time. Legend has it that Maymay Jo Lama, the Lama of the *Tshen* of Binakhar retires to meditate from the eighth of the third month to the eighth of the fourth month every year. And during that period, nobody was supposed to visit Binakhar. Should anybody break the rule, the *Tshen*- Maymay Jo Lama's follower, would send hell storms to all the neighbouring villages. The residents of Goenpakap and the other neighbouring villages had respected that rule for generations. If one must visit Binakhar during that period to retrieve some cattle or horses that often sneaked away into Binakhar to steal its lush green grass, one must first make an offering of wine and uncooked rice to Maymay Jo Lama, and apologise for the inconvenience. It was also said that if someone secretly visited Binakhar during that period, the residents of his as well as the neighbouring villages almost always knew that someone has broken the rule since they received unexpected hell storms.

When we reached Binakhar, the horses were not there. "I saw their foot marks on the way. Then, as we neared Binakhar I lost them. I guess I was not concentrating on tracking the horses," said my father. "But I am sure that they will be at Thomachen," he concluded optimistically. Thomachen was another community grazing land just about thirty minutes' walk from Binakhar. "I think you are tired of walking. Why don't you wait here and take a good rest while I go and get the horses. I will get back in a flash," suggested my father.

*S*ince there were no strawberries at Binakhar, I did not want to wait for him there. And why would there be any strawberries at that time anyway! It just was not the season. I had just assumed that there would always be strawberries at Binakhar since there were lot of them around the last time I had been there. Besides, Binakhar looked so deserted and lonely. However, I could not say 'No' to my father's suggestion so I just nodded to what he proposed.

He took me to one of the highest points of the grassland where he asked me to sit down on a rock. Then, he unsheathed his dragger and put it in my hand. "Hold on to this no matter what," he instructed me. "Do not put it away at any cost, you understand?" he added.

I nodded a 'Yes' and held on to the dragger with both hands.

"I will whistle like this," he said and blew a sharp whistle, "time and again so that you will know that I am not far away from you."

I nodded half-heartedly again as I regretted coming with him and longed to get out of Binakhar.

"Remember to stay put. Do not leave this rock," he instructed me.

As I sat on the rock and looked on, my father hurried down the slope and started to get smaller and smaller as the distance between us kept on increasing. As promised, he looked back towards me and kept on blowing a sharp whistle from time to time. After a while he disappeared from my view, and his whistle slowly became indiscernible. Then, I started to feel utterly lonely and more and more scared as the minutes flew, and began to hold on to the dragger even tighter. Then, suddenly, to my utmost relief I heard some footsteps and murmuring

And, I held onto the dragger tightly...

sound behind me. I quickly got up on my feet and turned around expecting to find some people behind me. But there was not a soul in sight within the reach of my vision across the vast grassland. I listened intently and the only thing that greeted me was a single gust of wind that blew hard into my face from nowhere. I turned back and looked down the slope for my father. Neither he was in sight nor his whistle in the air. Then, something hit me on my back. I turned back, and found out that it was a block of dry cow dung that had hit me. "Someone is trying to play planks on me," I thought aloud. "Please don't throw anymore cow dung at me, and come out of your hiding," I passed a solitary request.

Then, another two blocks of dry cow dung hit me on my back. Again I turned around and looked around. Then, instantly I realised that there was no place for anyone to hide from me. I was standing on one of the highest points of the grassland from where I could see everything. There just was not any place for a man to hide and throw cow dung at me. Suddenly, I knew that I had company- an invisible company who wanted to hurt me. And I held on to the dragger tightly and held it at an angle from my body like a swordsman ready to attack. No more cow dung.

After what seemed like eternity, my father's whistle could be heard again. After a while, I could even see the horses and my father hurrying up the slope towards me. When he finally reached the skyline where I was standing, he looked at my face that was drained of blood with a surprise, took the dragger from me, put it in the sheath, lifted me off my feet and held me close. "Are you alright?" he asked.

I looked at the cow dung on the ground and kept mum. Then, instantly the sky grew dark as the dark clouds from the mountains in the north raced towards the sky above Binakhar and shielded the sun's rays from reaching the surface of the grassland. Urgent flashes of lightening and a loud thunder followed this. Then, as we rushed out of Binakhar and entered the forest, hailstones, the size of pink bean seeds, fell hard on the trees above our heads.

When we reached home, I told my mother everything that had happened at Binakhar.

"I told you not to take Pema with you!" she complained to my father. "And how could you leave him all alone at Binakhar at this time of the year? He could have gotten kidnapped and hidden by the *Tshen!* Did you hear what he said about him getting attacked with cow dung?" she screamed.

"Calm down now. Pema was tired. I had no choice but to leave him there so that I could get the horses faster. Besides, I left my dragger with him, unsheathed and in his hands with clear instructions to him not to put it away at any cost," explained my father. "That should have kept the *Tshen* away," he added.

"But still how could you? It was all your fault that the *Tshen* attacked Jigmi. And, it was also your fault that the village has received such a heavy hailstorm. Your whistling did it. Yes, your whistles made the *Tshen* angry," she concluded. "You promised not to make any noise at Binakhar! And you whistled. What will the village people say if they find out that you were the one who had angered the *Tshen*, one of our most important Guardian Deities!"

"They will surely know if you keep on screaming at me like this," cautioned my father, and my mother surely kept quiet.

That night, my mother introduced me to the world of the *Tshen* kidnapping and hiding the mortals. She told me that once the *Tshen* has kidnapped a mortal, it was most often than not that the kidnapped is lost for life. She also said that even if people comb the whole world to rescue the kidnapped, he or she will not be found because the *Tshen* will make him or her invisible. "Of course, he or she will see the rescuers looking for him or her. Yes, he or she will even hear them call for him or her. However, the *Tshen* will make the person invisible so that the rescuers cannot see that person. Besides, even if the kidnapped called out at the rescuers to acknowledge his presence nearby, the rescuers will not hear his or her cries," she reasoned.

"What does the *Tshen* do with his captive?" I asked curiously.

"Well, the *Tshen* will make him a slave," she replied as a matter of fact. "Of course, the *Tshen* will feed and clothe the captive as well. However, when the captive touches the seemingly delicious food of pork, beef and rice, the food will actually be just a bunch of earthworm, which of course the captive will have no choice but to eat as his hunger gets better of him. So, he will be always hunger, and grow weaker and weaker by the hour. And the seemingly beautiful dresses of silk when touched upon by him will actually be just barks and leaves, so he will be just wearing his own cloth which will turn into rags as time goes on, and ultimately he will be forced to wear barks and leaves," she continued.

"I wouldn't like to be the one to get kidnapped by the *Tshen*," I said as my mother's tale sent a chill through me.

"No one would, Pema," she said. "But of course, sometimes if the captive's loved ones performed a lot of rituals to appease the *Tshen* and request him to release the captives, he will do so," she continued again. "But it is said that this is very rare," she concluded.

Then, she explained to me why my father had left his naked dragger in my hands at Binakhar. "The immortals and the supernatural usually wouldn't dare attack a mortal who is armed," she reasoned. "This is why a man's dragger is regarded as a talisman of security," she concluded. "They say even the *Dredpo* and the *Dredmo* wouldn't dare try to kidnap a woman or a man respectively if one is armed," she added.

"*Dredpo* and *Dredmo!*" I exclaimed moving closer to her. "They kidnap people as well? So they are like *Tshen* too?" I continued without giving her a chance to answer.

"Yes, they do. The *Dredpo* will always kidnap women and attack men while the *Dredmo* will always kidnap men and attack women. However, they are not like the *Tshen*. Although they are both the Guardian Deities of the mountains around Binakhar, the *Tshen* holds a higher position than they do. Besides, the *Tshen* is an immortal while the *Dredpo* and the *Dredmo* are mortals like us," she explained.

Thereafter, I decided never to go to Binakhar with my father if my mother objected to my going.

Well, that was nothing, I agree. But, how about what happened to Kenchomo? Well, Kenchomo was a forty years old widow of three daughters. Her daughters could not find her one fateful morning. They said that their mother had stayed at home the night before while they had gone to attend a religious ritual at a neighbour's and stayed up till about three in the morning dancing. When they reached home, their mother was not there.

However, they had not panicked since they assumed that she might have gone to a neighbour's to kill her boredom and might have decided to sleep over. However, when their mother did not show up by 10 A.M. in the morning, they had looked for her at every neighbour's house.

"Did you ladies have a fight last night?" asked Choden of Wangmo, Kenchomo's eldest daughter.

"No. Why?" asked Wangmo.

"Nothing," replied Choden turning away.

"What do you mean?"

"Well, I heard your mother crying last night," said Choden.

"Where?" asked a surprised Wangmo.

"At your place, where else!" answered Choden. "Don't tell me that you daughters have been making your mother cry!" added Choden with a tone of disapproval.

"Of course not," assured Wangmo.

"Then why was she crying at the top of her voice last night?" countered Choden.

"That's what I am wondering about as well. She was supposed to be in bed. When we left for Chozom's house she stayed at home because she wanted to go to bed," explained Wangmo.

"Well, I thought I even heard her calling for help," added Choden scratching her head. "But I could be wrong," she confessed. She scratched her again as if trying to think hard, and finally said, "I sure did hear her crying last night. Was she sick or something?"

"No. Even if she had become sick abruptly after we had left for Chozom's, she would have been at home when we got back," said a nervous Wangmo.

By noon the daughters gathered at their house. Three neighbours had reported of having heard their mother crying the night before, but nobody had any information about their mother's whereabouts. So, they decided to consult the astrologer.

"Some kind of an evil spirit of the dead has harmed your mother last night," said the astrologer after going through a page from a thin hand-written booklet. "She has been led out of her house against her will, and taken towards the north-east. You can still trace their track if you look for it right away. But I cannot tell you how," he concluded.

"Will we be able to find her?" asked the youngest daughter in between sobs.

"Honestly, I don't know," confessed the astrologer. "Place your faith in the Three Jewels, and go find the track and trace it before it is too late," he advised.

The daughters sought help from their neighbours, and the search began again- this time for the track, as advised by the astrologer, their mother and the evil spirit were supposed to have taken. They started from outside their house working towards Northeast. Sure enough, they found a track leading towards Northeast. There were clear signs of someone having created the path just a couple of hours back. The bushes consisting of mostly nettles, dogweed and marijuana plants were roughly separated and stamped upon as if something or someone had been dragged over or through them. At some place, there were also human blood either on the ground or on bushes and shrubs. At last, the trackers reached the Khomachu River that was about 2 hours' walk down the valley. There on the bank of the river on a large rock, they found the dress Kenchomo was wearing the night before. The dress was put on the rock as if the victim had gone for a swim in the turbulent river. The daughters cried uncontrollably as they realised what had happened to their mother. Then, the group searched almost two kilometres down river for the victim or her body. They found nothing of Kenchomo.

Since they neither found the victim nor her body, they decided to consult the shaman. When the shaman performed the ritual, he was first possessed by Kenchomo's spirit.

"The late shaman Tshetenla walked into my house after my daughters left for Chozom's house. He told me that he was there to take me with him. When I declined to follow him against his repeated request, he dragged me out of my house and down to the Khomachu River," said the possessed crying. "There he stripped me naked and pushed me into the river. When I was being swept away by the river, my head crashed against a rock, and then a whirlpool sucked me down and pushed me into a small cave under a gigantic rock in the middle of the river. I am still stuck there. I want help. Please get me out of the river," the possessed pleaded in exactly Kenchomo's voice.

She cried at the top of her voice adding more eeriness to the already creepy happenings of the night. The village people who had gathered there to witness the shaman's performance did not even dare to breath properly. "Please, help me," begged the possessed crying pathetically. "Look, he is coming to get me again," added the possessed pointing his long index finger at the door, and backing away towards the corner of the room.

At this, the crowd at the door panicked and ran away from the door. Then, the shaman stopped crying abruptly, and wore a completely different expression. He looked around the room as if looking for something or someone. Then, he sat down in front of the altar on the antique carpet, smiled and asked for a cup of wine. He bottomed up the cup of wine in a single gulp, and asked for a second helping. After he had drunk the second helping in another single gulp, he asked who Kenchomo's eldest daughter was, and summoned her to him. "There is nothing to worry about. Your mother is in good hands. She is a little lost but I am sure that she will soon feel at home with me," he assured Wangmo.

"Who are you, and what are you talking about?" asked a surprised Wangmo.

"So, you have not recognised me as yet!" exclaimed the possessed. "I am *Pao* Tshetenla," he said.

At this, there was a long murmur in the room, and almost everyone was terror-stricken. Then, as every hair on Wangmo's body rose, she lost her nerves and fainted.

"Surprised?" laughed the possessed. "Don't be. Soon I am going to be your stepfather. I am going to make your mother my second wife,"

There was another murmur in the room.

"Hush!" ordered the possessed intimidating the crowd with a sweep of his red bulging eyes over them. "No matter what you do, Kenchomo is going to be with me forever," declared the possessed.

"Please have mercy on Kenchomo and her daughters, and let her go," pleaded the Altar Attendant. "Please accept our wine, food and belongings, but let her go."

"Wine, food and belongings in exchange for Kenchomo!" screamed the man. "You think you can fool me that easily, you insolent fool? Don't you know that I am not like the other spirits who can be made happy by offering some food and wine or who can be scared away by some half educated lay monk? I am *Pao* Tshetenla, the greatest *Pao* that ever lived," flared the possessed.

"Apologies, Great *Pao*. Please accept my most sincere apologies for my mistakes," begged the Altar Attendant. "But please let me know what you want in exchange for Kenchomo?"

"Nothing," he laughed again. "Just Kenchomo," he added laughing even louder.

Then, suddenly the shaman slumped on the carpet and lay there panting as if he has just completed a thousand-mile run, and started to weep in a woman's voice.

"He has been possessed by a woman's spirit," announced the Altar Attendant.

"Please, save me he is trying to drag me away again," begged the possessed shaman in Kenchomo's voice again. Then suddenly as his yes fell on Sangaymo, he called out, "You!" pointed her index finger at her. "You could have saved me that morning when I was being dragged away by Tshetenla's spirit! I saw you milking your cow from just a few yards away. You did not heed my cries for help. Then, as I called out your name, Tshetenla gagged me, and continued to drag me down the valley. Please save me now," she pleaded.

Then, she called out the names of her daughters, friends and half a dozen other people and begged them to her help. Suddenly the shaman lay motionless on the floor in a pool of sweat, and there was utter silence. Instantly, the attendant pulled the motionless shaman up on his dangling legs, and set him up on the carpet. Slowly the shaman began to sit up on the throne, open his eyes, and ask for some wine.

"What happened?" was the only thing the shaman uttered before calling the ritual off.

That was that. They never found Kenchomo's body. Later it was widely rumoured that Tshetenla and Kenchomo's spirits possessed people together. It was also rumoured that one of the possessed has said that the two had gotten married. Even to this very day, whenever someone is possessed by Tshetenla's spirit, the host must offer wine and food to both of them. If not it is customary for the possessed to point his or her finger at an empty spot near him or her and say, "Please, give some to Kenchomo as well."

Well, let me narrate to you another incident somewhat related to the other tow tales about the clandestine foes. It happened one peaceful night not long ago. Every one in my village had either gone to bed or was preparing their beds when our neighbour Kuwamo's pathetic cries silenced even the village's most ferocious barking dogs. Every one in our house rushed to her help.

"Tempa... Tempa..." Kuwamo stammered.

"What is wrong with Tempa?" asked my father.

"He... he has been possessed," she replied hysterically.

"What do you mean? Where is he?" asked my father quizzically.

"He was behaving very weirdly since sundown. He was gritting his teeth time and again, and looking at us with bulging eyes without a word. Then suddenly he got out of bed and ran out of the house. Now he is gone,"

"Gone?"

"Yes. He ran down this road towards Mendiling," reported Kuwamo pointing towards the barely visible mule track a few blocks away from her house.

"Mendiling! *Lama kheno!*" exclaimed my mother getting hysterical.

My mother had heard many tales about a headless lady either waylaying or throwing sand and stones at any mortal who dared to pass through Mendiling alone after twilight. Therefore, she was dreaded of the very name of the place.

"Calm down now," ordered my father turning towards my mother. "She said 'towards Mendiling,' not 'to Mendiling.' And there is no reason as why Tempa would go to Mendiling at this hour of the night," he added.

"But didn't Kuwamo say that Tempa was gritting his teeth and..."

"That's enough," growled my father. "You don't you..."

"But she is right. I think Tempa has been possessed by the ghost of Mendiling," cried Kuwamo. "You know that the victim acts the way Tempa did when he or she is possessed by the..."

"Don't jump to conclusions, Kuwamo. Nothing is going to happen to Tempa," consoled my father. "As I was saying, why don't you take the children home while I try...." He paused as the torches and voices of others coming to Kuwamo's rescue distracted us. "... while we go look for Tempa," he suggested to my mother.

"I think I and the children will stay with Kuwamo and keep her company," countered my mother.

"That's a good idea," agreed my father.

"Anything wrong?" asked some men in unison as they gathered around us.

Kuwamo started to cry even more, and did not say a word; may be she was imagining the worst of the worst that could happen or would already have happened to her husband. So my father shared what little information he had on the incident with the others. And instantly about a dozen men formed a search party and ran towards Mendiling with their dry bamboo touches held high above their heads. They filled up the night with all kinds of noises- prayers sang aloud at the top of their voices, and calls for Tempa. But of course, they did not call him by his name. They called him by either uncle or brother. You see, my village folks never called at someone by his name at night, except while inside the house. They say that the evil spirits will harm that person if someone called out his or her name at night. So, anyone doing that will be inviting trouble for himself or herself.

We went into Kuwamo's house after the men had left in search of Tempa. Some women joined us as well. Then the village's astrologer dropped by, and the ladies requested him to find out what was wrong with Tempa. He hastily consulted a book, and reported that Tempa was under the evil influence of a powerful spirit from the south. He also said that if Tempa were not rescued before dawn, he would vanish for good. Then he made an offering of wine and rice to all the local guardian deities. And the long wait for the search party began. No one in the house, except the kids younger than me, went to bed till the first crow of the rooster when the search party finally arrived, but without Tempa. My family did not go home that night since my parents, being Kuwamo's closest neighbours, had to co-ordinate the additional rituals the lay monks performed the rest of the night for Tempa's return. As for Kuwamo, she never stopped crying. I could hear her sobs every time I woke up.

The night was over. The second group of search party had already returned, the dawn had left, the rituals were over and it was already time to start cooking lunch, but there was no sign of Tempa's return. And the whole village assumed that Tempa was gone for good. After all, that was the astrologer's prediction- if Tempa was not rescued before dawn, he will be gone for good. The wave of anguish had darkened the peaceful village as everyone anticipated the worst for Tempa, and felt utterly sorry for Tempa and his family. Then, at around noon while my mother was about to serve us lunch, we heard a lot of commotion outside Kuwamo's house. As my father rushed to the scene, we looked on from the window facing Kuwamo's house. And to our utmost surprise and relieve, there was Tempa surrounded by a group of people.

"Was he possessed by the..." my mother began as my father walked in.

"Yes, he surely was possessed," roared my father furiously before my mother could finish her question. "By *ara*. The fool had been drinking too much last night," reported my father. "The stupid rascal! How could he do such a thing!"

***

# Glossary

| | |
|---|---|
| *Achey* | Elder brother |
| *Aie* | Grandmother or old woman |
| *Ama* | Mother |
| *Apa* | Father |
| *Ara* | Locally brewed/distilled wine |
| *Awue* | Thief |
| *Ayee* | An expression equivalent to 'Ah' or 'Oh' |
| *Bangchang* | A local beer filtered directly from fermented malt |
| *Bangchu* | A circular bamboo basket with lid used to eat/pack rice from/in |
| *Brokpa* | Yak herder |
| *Bumo* | Girl (Tibetan) |
| *Dendreygi* | Like that (Tibetan) |
| *Dom* | Bear |
| *Dorchoed, Digsha, Shaju* | Names of different Buddhist scriptures learned by junior lay monks |
| *Dredmo* | Female Yeti |
| *Dredpo* | Male Yeti |
| *Drukpa* | Bhutanese |
| *Gho* | Bhutanese male's garment |
| *Ka, Kha, Ga, Nga* | First four letter of the Bhutanese alphabet |
| *Kadrenchey* | Thank you |
| *Kencho sum* | The Three Jewels- Buddha, Sanga and Dharma |
| *Khandoma* | An angel |
| *Kira* | Bhutanese lady's garment |
| *Koenyer* | Monastery Attendant/caretaker |
| *Kuchey* | Please (while begging) |
| *Lama* | A Buddhist priest |

| | |
|---|---|
| *Lama kheno* | An expression equivalent to 'Oh God' or meaning I take refuge in the *Lama* |
| *Lopon* | Teacher |
| *Maymay* | Grandfather or old man |
| *Nyen* | Bad or evil spell |
| *Nyendu* | Umbrella |
| *Nyenpa* | The bad one or the Evil spell caster |
| *Paaah,Zaaie,Waaie* | Expressions of astonishment and appreciation |
| *Palang* | A cylindrical container used to store wine (usually) and water |
| *Pao* | Shaman |
| *Shonlop* | Spelling |
| Sonam *apa* | Sonam's father |
| *Suja* | Salted butter tea |
| *Sutra* | Holy Scripture |
| *Tegu* | Bhutanese lady's broach |
| *Tendrel* | Omen (Tibetan) |
| *Thu* | Spell |
| *Tshechu* | Festival |
| *Tshen* | A demi-god Guardian Deity |
| *Tshidue* | Combination of letters of a word |
| *Tshongpa* | Businessman |
| *Tshongpon* | King of business or Great Business-man |
| *Tsipa* | Astrologer |
| *Wai* | Hey |
| *Wang* | Religious blessing ceremony |
| *Way rang drag ta* | You are the best |
| *Ya* | O.K. |